"I want every word set down."

At the Globe Theatre, Falconer drew me aside. "We must find a better vantage point for you, one where you will hear every word."

"The galleries?" I suggested.

"Among those overdressed fops? You might as well go right up on stage. No, I've a better spot for you. Come." He led me to the rear of the playhouse, to the players' entrance. The door stood ajar, and through the crack, I could just make out the lines being spoken on the stage.

"This is no better," I whispered.

"Not here. Up there." He pointed to the stairs beside us. "Through that door. Conceal yourself behind the curtains at the rear of the small balcony."

I gaped upward. "Up there? But—"

His hand closed painfully around my upper arm. "And mark me! No excuses this time. I want every word set down. Understood?"

⟫⟩◆⟨⟪

"Featuring sympathetic characters, an intriguing setting, and dark forces creating conflicts within Widge and around him, this historical novel makes an exciting introduction to the period and to Shakespearean theater."
—*Booklist*

⟫⟩◆⟨⟪

An ALA Best Book for Young
An *SLJ* Best Book of the Year
A *Smithsonian* Magazine Nota
Golden Kite Award List

OTHER PUFFIN BOOKS YOU MAY ENJOY

THE SHAKESPEARE STEALER

~

Gary Blackwood

PUFFIN BOOKS

PUFFIN BOOKS
Published by the Penguin Group
Penguin Putnam Books for Young Readers,
345 Hudson Street, New York, New York 10014, U.S.A.
Penguin Books Ltd, 27 Wrights Lane, London W8 5TZ, England
Penguin Books Australia Ltd, Ringwood, Victoria, Australia
Penguin Books Canada Ltd, 10 Alcorn Avenue, Toronto, Ontario, Canada M4V 3B2
Penguin Books (N.Z.) Ltd, 182-190 Wairau Road, Auckland 10, New Zealand

Penguin Books Ltd, Registered Offices: Harmondsworth, Middlesex, England

First published in the United States of America by Dutton Children's Books,
a member of Penguin Putnam Inc., 1998
Published by Puffin Books,
a division of Penguin Putnam Books for Young Readers, 2000

9 10 8

THE LIBRARY OF CONGRESS HAS CATALOGED THE DUTTON EDITION AS FOLLOWS:
Blackwood, Gary L.
The Shakespeare stealer / by Gary Blackwood.—1st ed.
p. cm.
Summary: A young orphan boy is ordered by his master to infiltrate Shakespeare's
acting troupe in order to steal the script of "Hamlet," but he discovers
instead the meaning of friendship and loyalty.
ISBN 0-525-45863-8
[1. Theater—Fiction. 2. Orphans—Fiction. 3. Actors and actresses—Fiction. 4. Great
Britain—History—Elizabeth, 1558–1603—Fiction. 5. Shakespeare, William,
1558–1603—Fiction.] I. Title.
PZ7.B5338Sh 1998 [Fic]—dc21 97-42987 CIP AC

Puffin Books ISBN 0-14-130595-9

Printed in the United States of America

For Tegan,
my only collaboration—
and a masterpiece

THE
SHAKESPEARE
STEALER

I never knew my mother or my father. As reliably as I can learn, my mother died the same year I was born, the year of our Lord 1587, the twenty-ninth of Queen Elizabeth's reign.

The name I carried with me throughout my youth was attached to me, more or less accidentally, by Mistress MacGregor of the orphanage. I was placed in her care by some neighbor. When she saw how small and frail I was, she exclaimed "*Och*, the poor little pigwidgeon!" From that unfortunate expression came the appellation of Widge, which stuck to me for years, like pitch. It might have been worse, of course. They might have called me Pig.

Of my life at the orphanage, I have made it a habit to recall as little as possible. The long and short of it is, it was an institution, and institutions are governed by expediency. Mistress MacGregor was not a bad woman, just an overburdened one. Occasionally she lost her temper and beat one of us, but for the most part we were not mistreated so much as neglected.

The money given us by the parish was not enough to keep one child properly clothed and fed, let alone six or seven. We depended mostly upon charity. When someone felt charitable, our bellies were relatively full. Otherwise, we dined on barley mush and wild greens. When times were hard for others, they were doubly so for us.

It was the dream of each child within those dreary walls that someday a real family would come and claim him. Preferably it would be his true parents—who were, of course, royalty—but any set would do. Or so we thought.

When I was seven years of age, my prospects changed, as some say they do every seven years of a person's life— the grand climateric, I have heard it called. That orphan's dream suddenly became a reality for me.

The rector from the nearby hamlet of Berwick came looking for an apprentice and, thanks to Mistress MacGregor's praise, settled on me. The man's name was Dr. Timothy Bright. His title was not a religious one but a medical one. He had studied physick at Cambridge and practiced in the city of London before coming north to Yorkshire.

Naturally I was grateful and eager to please. I did readily whatever was asked of me, and at first it seemed I had been

very fortunate. Dr. Bright and his wife were not affection-
ate toward me—nor, indeed, toward their own children.
But they gave me a comfortable place to sleep at one end of
the apothecary, the room where the doctor prepared his
medicines and infusions.

There was always some potion simmering over a pot of
burning pitch, and one of my duties was to tend to these.
The pitch fire kept the room reasonably warm. I took my
meals in the kitchen. Though the situation was hardly
what we orphans had secretly hoped for, it was more or less
what I had expected—with one exception. I was to be
taught to read and write, not only in English but in Latin,
and not only in Latin but also in a curious abbreviated language of Dr. Bright's own devising. *Charactery*, he called it.
It was, to use his own words, "an art of short, swift, and secret writing, by the which one may transcribe the spoken
word as rapidly as it issues from the tongue."

His object, I soon learned, was not to offer me an educa-
tion so much as to prepare me to be his assistant. I was to
keep his scientific notes for him, and to transcribe his
weekly sermons.

I had always been a quick student, but I was never
quick enough to suit the doctor. He had some idea that his
method of stenography could be learned in a matter of
mere months, and he meant to use me to prove it.

I was a sore disappointment to him. It was an awkward
system, and it took me a full year to become reasonably
adept, and another year before I could set down every word

without begging him to speak more slowly. This vexed him, for once his ample mouth was set in motion, he did not like to stop it. To his mind, of course, the fault lay not with his system but with me, for being so thickheaded.

I never saw him write anything in this short hand himself. I am inclined to think he never mastered it. As I grew confident with the system, I began to make my own small improvements in it—without the doctor's knowledge, of course. He was a vain man. Because he had once written a book, a dry treatise on melancholy, he felt the world should ever after make special allowances for him. He had written nothing since, so far as I knew, except his weekly sermons. And, as I was soon to discover, not always those.

When I was twelve, and could handle a horse as well as a plumbago pencil, the doctor set me off to neighboring parishes each Sabbath to copy other rectors' sermons. He meant, he said, to compile a book of the best ones. I believed him until one Sunday when the weather kept me home. I sat in on Dr. Bright's service and heard the very sermon I had transcribed at Dewsbury a fortnight before.

It did not prick my conscience to know that I had been doing something wrong. We were not given much instruction in right and wrong at the orphanage. As nearly as I could tell, Right was what benefited you, and anything which did you harm was Wrong.

My main concern was that I might be caught. I had never asked for any special consideration, but now I asked Dr. Bright, as humbly as I could, to be excused from the task. He blinked at me owlishly, as if not certain he had heard me properly. Then he scratched his long, red-veined nose and said, "You are my boy, and you will do exactly as I tell you."

He said it as though it were an unarguable fact of life. That discouraged me far more than any threat or show of anger could have done. And he was right. According to law, I was his property. I had to obey or be sent back to the orphanage. As Mistress Bright was fond of reminding me, prentices were easily come by and easily replaced. In truth, he had too much invested in me to dismiss me lightly. But he would not have hesitated to beat me, and heavily.

There was a popular saying to the effect that England is a paradise for women, a prison for servants, and a hell for horses. Prentices were too lowly to even deserve mention.

Eventually our sermon stealing was discovered. The wily old rector at Leeds noticed my feverish scribbling, and a small scandal ensued. Though Dr. Bright received only a mild reprimand from the church, he behaved as though his reputation were ruined. As usual, the blame fell squarely on my thin shoulders. My existence there, which had never been so much to begin with, went steadily downhill.

As I had so often done in my orphanage days, I began to wish for some savior to come by and, seeing at a glance my superior qualities, take me away.

In my more desperate moments, I even considered running away on my own. As I learned to read and transcribe such books as Holinshed's *Chronicles* and Ralegh's *Discov-*

ery of Guiana, I discovered that there was a whole world out there beyond Yorkshire, beyond England, and I longed to see it with my own eyes.

Up to now, my life had been bleak and limited, and it showed no sign of changing. In a new country such as Guiana, I imagined, or a city the size of London, there would be opportunities for a lad with a bit of wherewithal to make something of himself, something more than an orphan and a drudge. And yet I held no real hope of ever seeing anything beyond the bounds of Berwick. Indeed, the thought of leaving rather frightened me.

I was so ill-equipped to set out into that world alone. I could read and write, but I knew none of the skills needed to survive in the unfamiliar, perhaps hostile lands that lay beyond the fields and folds of our little parish. And so I waited, and worked, and wished.

If I had had any notion of what actually lay in store for me, I might not have wished so hard for it.

When I was fourteen, the grand climateric struck again, and my fortunes took a turn that made me actually long for the safety and security of the Brights' home.

In March, a stranger paid a visit to the rectory, but it was not some gentleman come to claim me as his heir. He was, in fact, no gentleman at all.

The doctor and I were in the apothecary when the housekeeper showed the stranger in. Though dark was almost upon us, we had not yet lighted the rush lights. The frugal doctor put that off as long as possible. The flickering flames of a pitch pot threw wavering, grotesque shadows upon the walls.

The stranger stood just inside the doorway, motionless and silent. He might have been taken for one of the shadows, or for some spectral figure—Death, or the devil—come to claim one of us. He was well over average height; a long, dark cloak of coarse fabric masked all his clothing save his high-heeled leather boots. He kept the hood of the cloak pulled forward, and it cast his face in shadow. The only feature I could make out was an unruly black beard, which curled over his collar. A bulge under the left side of his cloak hinted at some concealed object—a rapier, I guessed.

We all stood a long moment in a silence broken only by the sound of the potion boiling over its pot of flame. Dr. Bright blinked rapidly, as if coming awake, and snatched the clay vessel from the flame with a pair of tongs. Then he turned to the cloaked figure and said, with forced heartiness, "Now, then. How may I serve you, sir?"

The stranger stepped forward and reached under his cloak—for the rapier, I feared. But instead he drew out a small book bound in red leather. When he spoke, his voice was deep and hollow-sounding, befitting a spectre. "This is yours, is it not?"

Hesitantly, the doctor moved nearer and glanced at the volume. "Why, yes. Yes it is." I recognized it as well now. It was one of a small edition Dr. Bright had printed up the year before, with the abundant title, *Charactery: An Art of Short, Swift, and Secret Writing*.

"Does it work?"

"I beg your pardon?"

"The system," the man said irritably. "Does it work?"

"Of course it works," Dr. Bright replied indignantly. "With my system, one may without effort transcribe the written or the spoken word—"

"How long does it take?" the man interrupted.

Dr. Bright blinked at him. "Why, as I was about to say, one may set down speech as rapidly as it is spoken."

The man gestured impatiently, as if waving the doctor's words aside. "How long to *learn* it?"

The doctor glanced at me and cleared his throat. "Well, that depends on the aptitude of the—"

"How *long*?"

The doctor shrugged. "Two months, perhaps. Perhaps more." Perhaps a lot more, I thought.

The stranger flung the book onto the trestle table, which held the doctor's equipment. A glass vessel fell to the floor and shattered.

"Now see here—" Dr. Bright began. But the man had turned away, his long cloak swirling so violently that the flame in the pitch pot guttered and smoked. He stood facing away a moment, as if deep in thought. I busied myself cleaning up the broken beaker, content for once to be a lowly prentice with no hand in this business.

The black-bearded stranger turned back, his face still shadowed and unreadable. "To how many have you taught this system of yours?"

"Let me see . . . There's my boy, Widge, here, and then—"

"How many?

"Well . . . one, actually."

The hooded countenance turned on me. "How well has he learned it?"

Dr. Bright assumed his false heartiness again. "Oh, perfectly," he said, to my surprise. He had never before allowed that I was anything more than adequate.

"Show me," the man said, whether to me or the doctor I could not tell. I stood holding the shards of glass in my hand.

"Are you quite deaf?" the doctor demanded. "The gentleman wishes a demonstration of your skill."

I set the glass in a heap on the table, then picked up my small table-book and plumbago pencil. "What must I write?"

"Write this," the stranger said. "I hereby convey to the bearer of this paper the services of my former apprentice—" The man paused.

"Go on," I said. "I've kept up wi' you." I was so intent on transcribing correctly and speedily that I'd paid no attention to the sense of the words.

"Your name," the man said.

"Eh?"

"What is your *name*?"

"It's Widge," the doctor answered for me, then laughed nervously, as if suddenly aware how odd was the name he had been calling me for seven years.

The stranger did not share his amusement. "—my former apprentice, Widge, in consideration of which I have accepted the amount of ten pounds sterling." He paused again, and I looked up. For some reason, Dr. Bright was staring openmouthed, seemingly struck dumb.

"Is that all?" I asked.

The man held out an unexpectedly soft and well-manicured hand. "Let me see it." I handed him the table-book. He turned it toward the light. "You have copied down every word?" I could not see the expression on his face, but I fancied his voice held a hint of surprise.

"Aye."

He thrust the table-book into my hand. "Read it back to me."

To the unschooled eye, the scribbles would have been wholly mysterious and indecipherable:

Yet I read it back to him without pause, and this time I was struck by the import of the words. "Do you—does this mean—?" I looked to Dr. Bright for an explanation, but he avoided my gaze.

"Copy it out now in a normal hand," the stranger said.

"But I—"

"Go on!" the doctor snapped. "Do as he says."

It was useless to protest. What feeble objection of mine could carry the weight of ten pounds of currency? I doubted the doctor earned that much in a year. Swallowing hard, I copied out the message in my best hand, as slowly as I reasonably might. Meantime my brain raced, searching for some way to avoid being handed over to this cold and menacing stranger.

Whatever the miseries of my life with the Brights, they were at least familiar miseries. To go off with this man was to be dragged into the unknown. A part of me longed for new places, new experiences. But a larger part clung to the security of the familiar, as a sailor cast adrift might cling fast to any rock, no matter how small or barren.

Briefly, I considered fleeing, but that was pointless. Even if I could escape them, where would I go? At last I came to the end of the message and gave it up to Dr. Bright, who appended his signature, then stood folding the paper carefully. I knew him well enough to know that he was waiting to see the color of the man's money.

In truth, I suppose I knew him better than I knew anyone in the world. It was a sad thought, and even sadder to think that, after seven years, he could just hand me over to someone he had never before met, someone whose name he did not know, someone whose face he had never even seen.

The stranger drew out a leather pouch and shook ten gold sovereigns from it onto the table. As he bent nearer the light of the pitch pot, I caught my first glimpse of his features. Dark, heavy brows met at the bridge of a long, hooked nose. On his left cheek, an ugly raised scar ran all the way from the corner of his eye into the depths of his dark beard. I must have gasped at the sight of it, for he turned toward me, throwing his face into shadow again.

He thrust the signed paper into the wallet at his belt, revealing for an instant the ornate handle of his rapier. "If you have anything to take along, you'd best fetch it now, boy."

It took even less time to gather up my belongings than it had for my life to be signed away. All I owned was the small dagger I used for eating; a linen tunic and woollen stockings I wore only on the Sabbath; a worn leather wallet containing money received each year on the anniversary of my birth—or as near it as could be determined; and an ill-fitting sheepskin doublet handed down from Dr. Bright's son. It was little enough to show for fourteen years on this Earth.

Yet, all in all, I was more fortunate than many of my fellow orphans. Those who were unsound of mind or body were still at the orphanage. Others had died there.

I tied up my possessions with a length of cord and returned to where the men waited. Dr. Bright fidgeted with the sovereigns, as though worried that they might be taken back. The stranger stood as still and silent as a figure carved of wood.

When he moved, it was to take me roughly by the arm and usher me toward the door. "Keep a close eye on him, now," the doctor called after us. I thought it was his way of expressing concern for my welfare. Then he added, "He can be sluggish if you don't stir him from time to time with a stick."

The stranger pushed me out the front door and closed it behind him. A thin rain had begun to fall. I hunched my shoulders against it and looked about for a wagon or carriage. There was none, only a single horse at the snubbing post. The stranger untied the animal and swung into the saddle. "I've only the one mount. You'll have to walk." He pulled the horse's head about and started off down the road.

I lingered a moment and turned to look back at the rectory. The windows were lighted now against the gathering dark. I half hoped someone from the household might be watching my departure, and might wish me Godspeed, and I could bid farewell in return before I left this place behind forever. There was no one, only the placid tabby cat gazing at me from under the shelter of the eaves.

"God buy you, then," I told the cat and, slinging my bundle over my shoulder, turned and hurried off after my new master.

3

I had no notion of where I was being taken. We headed south out of Berwick, past the slate-roofed house of Mr. Cheyney, the wool merchant, past the old mill, past the common fields. I had been south as far as Wakefield; beyond that, my geography was unreliable. I knew that if one continued south a week or so, one would end up in the vicinity of London. But I was sure this man was no Londoner.

Judging from Dr. Bright's accounts, the men of London dressed in splendid clothing, all ornamented and embroidered, and spoke in a civil and cultured manner. They lived in houses ten times larger and grander than Mr. Cheyney's and consorted with ladies of elegance and beauty.

I had a hard time matching the stranger's pace. He never

looked back to see whether I was keeping up, or whether I was following at all. Yet I was sure that, if I took it into my head to slip off into the dark woods, he would know at once. Besides, there were the woods themselves to be reckoned with.

About Berwick, the woods were tame. The trees were broad and widely spaced; sheep and pigs grazed on the swards among them, and on my rare free afternoon, I had walked there without fear.

These woods were dense and dark and dreadful. To run there would be like jumping into the fire to escape the cooking pot. Those trees, I had heard, concealed every unsavory brigand and every ravenous beast of prey in the shire—until nightfall, when they ventured out upon roads such as this, in search of victims.

I shuddered and, breaking into a trot, closed the gap between myself and the stranger's horse. When I grasped the frame of his saddle, I could shuffle along with less effort. Still, I was not used to physical exertion, and the pace took its toll on me. I summoned enough breath to say, "Will we be stopping for the night, then?"

The man twisted in his saddle and glanced down at my hand clutching the frame. I was afraid he might push me away, but he faced front again. "Speak when you are spoken to," he said in a low voice.

We pushed on long after the last light was gone from the watery sky. I hoped that we might put up at the King's Head in Wakefield, but we passed by without pausing.

From there, the road was unfamiliar to me, though its ruts and rocks felt all too familiar. The bottoms of my shoes, which were thin as paper, grew ragged. At last I trod on a sharp stone that pierced the leather sole, and the sole of my foot as well. "Gog's blood!" Losing my grip on the saddle, I fell to my knees on the hard dirt.

The stranger wheeled his horse about. "Silence!" he hissed. "You'll have every cutpurse within a league down upon us!"

"Sorry!" I whispered. "I've hurt meself."

He sighed in disgust. "Can you walk?"

I tried to place my weight on the injured foot. It was like stepping on a knife. "I wis not."

"If I give you the flat of my blade, can you?"

I considered a moment, then took a sharp breath. "Nay, I still wis not."

He reached out for me, and instinctively, I ducked. "Give me your hand!" His voice was harsh and impatient. Hesitantly, I put my hand in his. Despite the clammy air, his palm was hot and dry, like that of a man with a fever, and his grip was painfully strong. He lifted me bodily and dragged me across the horse's flank until I could swing one leg over the animal's haunches. I had scarcely settled in before we were off again, at a quicker gait than before. I dropped my bundle in my lap and clung desperately to the saddle frame.

After a time, I relaxed a bit, and even felt drowsy. My head drooped forward and came to rest on the stranger's damp cloak. He jerked violently, as though bitten, and I sat abruptly erect again. Despite all my care, this happened several more times. Finally, the man snapped, "Either ride properly, or go back to shank's mare"—meaning, of course, my feet.

As the night advanced, the air grew more chill, which helped keep me uncomfortably awake. In the small hours, we came upon an inn. My master took a room; I was given a pallet on the floor and was wakened long before I was ready the following morning. A loaf of bread and some cheese served as both breakfast and dinner. Each was eaten unceremoniously upon the back of the horse.

We paused once in the afternoon, to allow the animal to drink from a stream. I barely had time to soak my swollen foot before we were again on our way. When night fell, we were once more beset by woods on either hand, and no settlement in sight before or behind. What drove this man so, I wondered, to risk his life—and mine—on the high road after dark? Were we too near the end of our journey to stop?

All the preceding night and day, I had been in a sort of daze, brought on by the abrupt change in my circumstances. Now I was beginning to come out of it, and a hundred thoughts and questions rose in me, none of which I dared give voice to. All I could do was what I had always done: wait and watch and hope for the best.

The trees edged in and threatened to claim the very road. In places, their branches met above our heads and interlaced, nearly blocking out the light of the half moon. In one such dismal spot we got our first taste of trouble. There was no warning; one moment the road was deserted, dappled with moonlight, the next, half a dozen shadowy figures stood before us. I stiffened, and a gasp escaped me.

Instead of turning back or spurring the horse in a bid for escape, the stranger reined in and slowly approached the bandits, who stood in a crescent, blocking the path. Most were armed only with staves and short swords, but one man of imposing stature held a crossbow leveled at us. "Hold!"

The stranger let his horse advance until we were nearly abreast of the big man. "God rest you, gentlemen," he said, in a surprisingly amiable tone.

The big man, crowded by our horse, let his crossbow drift to one side. "Don't tell me you're a parson."

"Far from it."

"Good. I don't like doing business with parsons. They're too parsimonious." He guffawed at his own joke. "Well, let's have it, then."

"Have what?" the stranger asked innocently.

The big man laughed again, and this time his companions joined in. "Have what? 'a says. Have what? Why have a pot of ale wi' us, of course." More soberly, the man said, "Come now, enough pleasantries. Let's have your purse."

The stranger reached inside his cloak and drew out the

purse with which he had bought me. It was still heavy with coins. "Forgive me for not taking your meaning."

"Oh, aye," the big man said. "An you forgive us for taking your money."

The stranger leaned down, as if to surrender the pouch. But instead he swung it in a sudden arc and struck the bandit full in the face. The man staggered backward; his crossbow loosed its bolt, which flew wild. I gave a cry of dismay as the other thieves sprang forward.

But the stranger was ready. The hand that had held the purse an instant before now grasped his rapier. He kicked the nearest man's stave aside and give him a quick thrust to the throat. A second man's sword he deflected with his cloak, and sent the man reeling away, clutching at his bloody face. He seized the blade of a third man's weapon in his cloak-wrapped hand and yanked it away.

I, meantime, was struggling with a one-armed ruffian who had latched on to my tunic and was trying to pull me to the ground. I clung tenaciously to the saddle frame and kicked at my assailant, but it was no use. My small strength gave out, and I toppled like a wounded bird from my perch.

Flailing about for something to break my fall, I fastened on the neck of the one-armed man. He cursed and stumbled backward, and we both crashed to the ground. A rock struck my elbow, numbing my arm. It did even more damage to the bandit's head, and he lay suddenly still.

I dragged my limp arm free and got to my feet to see the

stranger dispatch the last of the outlaws with a sweeping blow that knocked the man into the road, where his companions lay in various attitudes and degrees of unconsciousness.

The stranger guided the horse to where the crossbow lay. With a flick of his blade, he severed its string, then lifted his fallen purse with the point of the sword. He shook a single coin from it and tossed it at the feet of the big man, who sat ruefully holding his jaw. "If this is a toll road, you might simply have tolled me."

The big man let out an abrupt laugh, then groaned with pain. "Would that you had been a parson after all."

Several of the bandits had begun to come around now. "Could we go on?" I pleaded. The stranger twisted about impatiently and, grasping the back of my tunic, hoisted me up behind him. Though I kept a wary eye on the thieves, he did not deign to glance back even once. Only when they were well out of sight did I breathe easily again. "What you did back there—I've never seen the like."

The stranger was silent a long moment, then he said gruffly, "You were told not to speak unless spoken to."

We rode on until at last, dew damp and bone weary, we came upon a small inn, where we took a room for what remained of the night. In the morning, after breaking fast with cold beef and ale, we set out once more, still heading south. My thighs were chafed raw from the constant motion of the horse, and every sinew and muscle ached fiercely.

About midday, I got up enough courage to ask, "When will we be there?"

The stranger gave me a glowering glance. "We will be there when we get there." Even in daylight, I saw little of his face, for he never pulled back the hood, except by accident. I did, however, memorize every square inch of the back of his cloak.

I despaired of that day ever reaching its end, but of course it did, and with it our journey. Just as the sun rounded the corners of the Earth, we came around a bend in the road and before us lay a landscape of stark steeples and thatched roofs glowing golden in the last rays of the sun—more buildings than I had ever seen in one place. "Is this London, then?" I asked, forgetting in my astonishment the commandment to hold my tongue.

Unexpectedly, the stranger laughed. "Hardly. It's only Leicester."

"I've heard of that," I said, feeling like an ignorant lumpkin.

Before we quite entered the town, we turned off the road and down a narrow lane to a substantial house surrounded by a high hedge. The stranger guided our horse down a cobbled walk to a stable nearly as imposing as the house.

I was scarcely able to believe that we had reached our destination, but the stranger dismounted and snapped, "Don't sit there like a dolt; get down!" My legs were in such a condition that they buckled under me. The stranger seized my arm and all but dragged me to the rear of the house.

As we came around the corner, we nearly collided with a husky youth who was headed for the stable. He stepped aside quickly and bobbed his head apologetically. "You're back, then. I'll see to your horse, sir."

"Give her an extra ration of oats. She's had a hard trip."

"Right, sir." The boy tried to be on his way, but the master stopped him.

"Adam."

"Yes, sir?"

"Your place is in the stable. Stay out of the kitchen."

"I will, sir." He hurried off.

"Lazy swad," the man muttered. We entered a spacious kitchen, lit not by rush lights but by actual candles. A plain young woman in a linen apron and cap was busy at the fireplace. "We'll be wanting supper, Libby," the man told her. "The boy will have his in his room."

"The garret?" the girl asked.

The man nodded brusquely, turned, and was gone.

The girl looked me over curiously. "Where are you from?"

"Berwick-in-Elmet."

She raised her eyebrows as though I'd said I came from the Antipodes. "Where's *that*?"

"Up Yorkshire way. Near Leeds."

"I see," she said, as if that explained something—my appearance, perhaps, or my speech. "Well, come. Best get you to your room."

"I'm to have a room of me own?"

"It looks that way, don't it?" She picked up a candle and led me through the pantry and up a set of steps, which in my exhaustion I was hard put to climb, to a small attic room. "Here you are. It's not much."

It could have been a pit full of snakes for all I cared. The moment she was gone, I blew out the candle and collapsed on the bed. I expected to be shaken awake at the crack of dawn, but when I finally woke, the sun was streaming through the gabled windows. I leaped up, hardly knowing where I was, struck my head on the low ceiling, and sat down again. For several minutes I remained there, holding my head and letting my mind adjust to these new and strange surroundings.

A pewter bowl of cold meat, carrots, and potatoes sat beside the bed. I gobbled it in a trice, then tried standing again. My legs felt uncertain, and my foot still pained me. Hearing footfalls on the stairs, I straightened myself and tried to look as though I had been up for hours and awaiting my master's call. But my visitor was only the stableboy. He thrust my bundle of clothing into my arms. "I'd put on something clean if I was you," he said. "You smell."

It seemed wicked to don my Sunday garb on an ordinary day, but it was all I had. The bundle had been tampered with, untied and hastily retied. I spread the clothing out on my bed and found my wallet, which had contained my meager savings. The money was gone, every farthing.

Though I was sure it was the stableboy's doing, I knew better than to say so. I was the new boy here, and I had long since learned that new boys have no rights. I would have to content myself with cursing him roundly and silently.

When I carried my dirty clothing downstairs, the girl

called Libby took them and gingerly dropped them in a basket. "The master said to bring you to him as soon as you were up, but I expect you'll want to be fed first."

"I've eaten. What was in the bowl."

She clucked her tongue. "That was last night's supper, you ninny. You were asleep when I brought it up."

I shrugged. "It served well enough as breakfast."

"Dinner, more like. It's nearly noon. Come, then."

As we passed from the kitchen into a great open room, I said, "Will 'a be cross wi' me, do you wis?"

She cast me the same doubtful glance she'd given when I told her where I hailed from. *"Wis?"*

"Aye," I said, wondering what she found so strange in a word I'd used all my life.

Libby led me up a wide staircase, to a large gallery with a dozen windows, and tapestries hung between them. "I can't say whether he'll be cross or no. He's a queer one, the master is." She turned and whispered, "Not to tell him I said so, now."

I made a cross over my heart as proof that I would not. We stopped before a paneled door, on which the girl knocked lightly. "Enter!" called a voice from within. The girl motioned me inside. As Libby pushed the door shut, she sent me an encouraging wink.

The room in which I found myself was so foreign that I might have stepped into another land. A soft carpet covered the floor; two of the paneled walls were hung with pictures; the other two were obscured top to bottom by more books than I would have suspected existed in all of England. If this is but Leicester, I thought, what must London be like?

So awed was I that it was a moment before my eyes fell on the figure at the writing desk, bent over some close task. "Widge?" he said, without turning.

I swallowed nervously. "Aye."

"Come, sit down." I was almost at the man's side before he looked up from his papers. I stared dumbly at him. This was not the fearsome stranger who had brought me here. This was a mild-looking man with a well-trimmed beard and a balding head of hair of an odd, reddish hue. He smiled slightly at my obvious bewilderment. "My name is Simon Bass," he said. "I am your new master."

"Y̶ou might sit down," Simon Bass said, "before you fall down."

I sank into an upholstered chair. "But—but I thought—"

"You thought the one who brought you here was to be your master." Bass shrugged. "Falconer is not the most communicative of men, nor the most genial. But he is reliable, and effective. I could not go to Yorkshire myself because . . . well, for various reasons. He got you here in one piece, at any rate."

"Aye . . . mostly."

Bass chuckled. "Neither is Falconer the most considerate of traveling companions, I warrant. Have you eaten?"

"Aye."

"Good. Good." He shoved his papers aside, took up a

pipe, and filled the bowl of it with tobacco from an earth-enware jar. "Then we can get right down to business. You'll be wanting to know what's expected of you."

"Aye." Though my seat was comfortable, I shifted about nervously.

"Very well." He went to the fireplace, touched a taper to a live coal, and lit the pipe. "The first thing I expect is that you say 'yes' rather than 'aye.' Your task will not require you to speak overmuch, but I'd as soon you did not brand yourself as a complete rustic. Understood?"

"Aye—I mean, yes."

"Excellent." His manner, which had become prickly, turned cordial again. "Now. When you go to London—"

"London?"

"Yes, yes, London. It's a large city to the south of here."

"I ken that, but—"

"Let me finish, then ask questions. When you go to London, you will attend a performance of a play called *The Tragedy of Hamlet, Prince of Denmark*. You will copy it in Dr. Bright's 'charactery' and you will deliver it to me. Now. Any questions?"

I scarcely knew where to begin. "I—well, how—that is—they will not object? The men who present the play?"

"Only if they discover you. Naturally you will be as surreptitious as possible."

"And an they do discover me?" I asked, thinking of the sermon-copying affair.

Bass blew out a cloud of smoke which made me cough.

"The Globe's audience is customarily between five hundred and one thousand. Do you suppose they can watch over every member of it?"

"I wis not."

"You *wis* not. Of course they can't. You will use a small table-book, easily concealed." He rummaged through the riot of papers on his writing desk. "You see how easily it is concealed? Even I can't find it." Finally he came up with a bound pad of paper the size of his hand. "There. Keep it in your wallet. You have a plumbago pencil?"

"Ay—yes."

"Any further questions?"

"An I might ask . . . for what purpose am I to do this?"

Bass turned a penetrating look on me. "Does it matter?"

"Nay, I wis not. I was only curious."

He nodded and scratched the balding top of his head. "You'll know sooner or later, I suppose." He puffed thoughtfully at his pipe, then continued. "I am a man of business, Widge, and one of my more profitable ventures is a company of players. They are not nearly so successful as the Lord Chamberlain's or the Admiral's Men, but they do a respectable business here in the Midlands. As they have no competent poet of their own, they make do with hand-me-downs, so well used as to be threadbare. If they could stage a current work, by a poet of some reputation, they could double their box."

"Box?"

"The money they take in. And my profit would also double. Now someone, sooner or later, will pry this *Tragedy of Hamlet* from the hands of its poet, Mr. Shakespeare, just as they did *Romeo and Juliet* and *Titus Andronicus.*" He jabbed his pipe stem at me for emphasis. "I would like it to be us, and I would like it to be now, while it is new enough to be a novelty. Besides, if we wait for others to obtain it, they will do a botched job, patched together from various sources, none of them reliable. Mr. Shakespeare deserves better; he is a poet of quality, perhaps of genius, and if his work is to be appropriated, it ought to be done well. That is your mission. If you fulfill it satisfactorily, the rewards will be considerable. If you do not—" He gave a wry smile. "Well, Falconer will make certain that you do."

The anticipation that had been growing in me turned suddenly sour. "I—I did not ken 'a would go wi' me."

Bass laughed. "Did you suppose I would send you off to London on your own? You can't even speak the language properly. I might just as well send you to Guiana." He patted one of my sagging shoulders. "Don't look so inconsolable. Falconer will take good care of you, and you can learn a lot from him. Besides, looking on the bright side, this time you'll have a horse of your own."

So the room that was to be mine was mine for two nights only. The following morning, we set out for London.

Though my legs had not quite recovered, by shortening my stirrups and leaning back in the saddle, I could ride without too much discomfort.

Naturally, Falconer set a brisk pace. Mr. Bass had no doubt instructed him not to delay, and he, in his fanatical fashion, took this to mean that we should drive our mounts and ourselves to exhaustion.

I was better fed this time, for Libby had provided me with all manner of victuals—fruit, meat pies, clapbread. She had also found time to wash and mend my workaday clothing, and patch my torn shoe. When I thanked her, she had waved my words away. "Tush, it's no more than is expected of me. Don't you go getting yourself into trouble in the city, now."

Trouble? I thought. In London? Ever since I could remember, I had heard Dr. Bright and others speak of London in tones usually reserved for talk of the Heavenly City. As the Earth was the center of the greater universe, so London was the center of our miniature universe. And I, Widge, orphan and lowly apprentice, was moving toward that center.

Sore legs be damned. I dug my heels into my horse's ribs and urged her into a gait that, for a short time, outstripped even Falconer. I had gone no more than a mile when a hare scampered from the brush and across the roadway. My mount reared, nearly spilling me from the saddle. Falconer came abreast of me. "What's the trouble?" he demanded.

"A hare," I said, shaken. " 'A ran across me path."

"That's all? From your face, anyone would guess it was a dragon at least."

"Do you not ken it's a bad omen?"

"I take no stock in omens. Men make their own fates."

"Not prentices," I muttered. I urged my horse forward, but not with quite the same eagerness as before.

6

*D*espite our haste, it took us two full days to reach London. Our passage was uneventful, and our conversation limited. We slept the night in Bedford, and in late afteroon of the following day, I first caught sight of the rooftops of the great city on the Thames.

The volume of traffic had swelled threefold. We passed carts and wagons of every size and description—full ones on their way into the city, empty ones coming back. Apparently, London had an enormous appetite for goods of every kind, from livestock and vegetables to timber and stone. In my poor parish, most of what we used came from the farms roundabout. It was curious to think of carting in food and materials from all over the country.

We approached the city on Aldersgate Street. All around

us lay fields and orchards; I might have imagined I had never left home had I not looked dead ahead, where the thousand buildings of the city, with their red tile roofs, lay ranged in rows within the ancient stone wall, so densely packed that those which lined the river seemed about to be nudged into it by those on the hill above.

"Close your mouth," Falconer said, "before your soul flies out."

Embarrassed, I clamped my mouth shut and urged my horse forward. By the time we passed through the wall at Aldersgate, the sun had set, and the streets were growing dark. There was much less bustle and clamor than I had expected. I was, in truth, a bit disappointed.

We had gone no more than a hundred yards before a man carrying a pikestaff and a bell and leading a mastiff on a leash stalked up to us. "You're to lead your horses within the walls!"

Falconer reined in. I watched him anxiously, wondering how he would respond to this order. To my surprise, he swung from his saddle without a word, though his bearing spoke of resentment and disdain, and walked on, leading his mount. I dropped to the cobblestones and hurried after.

My eyes were on Falconer, not on my footing. I stumbled into a deep depression in the ground and landed painfully on one knee. The watchman burst out laughing. "You're a green one, an't you?"

I was tempted to reply that, where I came from, we did

37

not leave holes in the street for people to fall into. But I thought better of it and limped off with my horse in tow. Now I saw that the depression was in fact a ditch that ran the length of the street. I also became aware of the noisome stench arising from it.

Falconer growled, "Must I watch you every moment, like an errant sheep?"

"I couldn't help it. I fell in that ditch."

"Then you have reason to act sheepish. That's the sewer." He waved a hand at me, as though to keep me at a distance. "Be sure you walk downwind of me from here on."

I saw at once that Falconer was no stranger to London. He made his way through the streets with such an air of assurance, indeed of arrogance, that those few townfolk still abroad gave him a wide berth—or perhaps it was due to the air about *me*.

Even in the dark, the buildings that towered over us were impressive. Some were a full four storeys high; in one block, the fronts of the buildings were decorated with beaten gold. To our right, a huge cathedral was silhouetted against the rising moon. As I stared at it, the bells in its square steeple rang the hour of compline.

"Stop gawking, and move your pins!" Falconer called. "That's the curfew bell!"

"London has a curfew?" I asked incredulously. The largest and most cosmopolitan city in England, the symbol of freedom to thousands upon thousands of country youths, compelled its citizens to be off the streets at nine o'clock?

Falconer strode on without replying. We passed the public stocks, which were empty, then came upon a spot where three streets diverged, like a trident. Falconer took the right-hand prong, and we walked another several blocks before we stopped under a sign which depicted St. George slaying a rather pitiful-looking dragon. "This will be our lodgings," Falconer said. "If we should become separated, find your way here. Just ask anyone for The George, near the Four Corners. Understood?"

"Aye. The George, near the Four Corners."

"Otherwise you are to talk to no one. Is *that* understood?"

"Aye."

He handed me the reins of his mount. "Take the horses through that archway to the stable." I started off, but his voice made me turn back. "One more thing."

"Aye?"

"Stop saying aye."

"I will," I promised. *Yes*, I told myself as I led the horses into the courtyard. Not aye, yes. Yes, yes, yes. Anything that would make me appear more like a Londoner and less like a green country woodcock, I was more than willing to adopt. But if I truly did not wish to be sniggered at, my first task would have to be to change my reeking clothing.

The main room of the inn, where we supped, was enormous, with a wide fireplace and half a dozen massive tables. At each sat four or five patrons, some eating, some drinking, some playing at dice.

As I sat opposite Falconer, gobbling my bread and herring, a quarrel kindled among the dice players. Two men sprang to their feet, their hands reaching for their rapiers, but a third man stepped between them. There was a moment's heated discussion, then one of the antagonists stalked from the room, wearing a grim look. Falconer seemed to take no notice of the scene. "There was nearly a fight!" I whispered.

"There will be one yet," he said. "They've merely chosen another time and place."

"You mean a duel? Over a game of dice?"

He shrugged, and his hood moved a little, revealing the long scar that traversed his cheek. "Some men will fight over nearly anything."

We finished our supper in silence. When Falconer started up to his room, I hastened after him. He waved me away with an impatient gesture, as if I still stank, though I had done my best to wash thoroughly. "You will make your bed in the stables, boy."

I backed away, surprised and a bit hurt. Simon Bass had led me to believe that my part in this "mission," as he had called it, was an important one. But to Falconer I was apparently no more than an unskilled and incompetent prentice, not fit to converse with or share a room with. In truth I was, except perhaps for my diet, no better than his horses.

For three days we sat idle at the inn, waiting for the

Lord Chamberlain's men to perform *The Tragedy of Hamlet*. There was a different play each afternoon, and *Hamlet* would not be presented until Tuesday. I spent much of the time watching the traffic that thronged the streets. Every conceivable conveyance passed by, from rude carts to fine coaches, and every conceivable class of person: ragged street urchins begging for farthings; fat merchants in sensible clothing; young dandies in doublets so extravagantly slit and slashed as to appear ready to fall off; dozens of prentices my age or younger, all wearing the same style of woollen cap.

The cries of street vendors mingled in a kind of exotic music: "Quick periwinkles, quick, quick!" "Fine Seville oranges, fine lemons." "I ha' ripe cowcumbers, ripe!" "Sweep! Chimbly sweep, mistress, from bottom to top. No soot shall then fall in your porridge pot!" "Ha' you any rats, mice, polecats, or weasels, or any old cows sick o' the measles?" I occupied several hours transcribing these cries, partly because they were so colorful, partly to exercise my stenography.

I had never witnessed a play, except for a few short interludes played on the bed of a wagon in the town square at May festival, so I had little idea of what to expect. How long would the performance last? Half an hour? Six hours? How rapidly would the players speak? What about their actions; should I transcribe them as well? What if they recited in Latin, or Greek?

I longed to ask Falconer all these things, but I knew

what his reply would be. He would glare at me and tell me to wait and see. So I sat about the courtyard and the stable, and like a good prentice, I waited.

On Tuesday, after a midday meal of fried fish and oysters, we set out for the theatre. We followed a narrow, unpaved street downhill to the Thames, and I was suddenly presented with a whole different aspect of the city.

Here were no gold-plated buildings or great cathedrals, only shabby rows of houses, cheek by jowl. With no space to spread sidewise, they had arched over the street, like the trees on that desolate stretch of road where we had met the outlaws, nearly meeting above our heads, shutting out the sun.

There were no street vendors here, nor prosperous merchants, only sullen wives emptying their slop jars into the street, sometimes missing the scrawny, shoeless children playing there, sometimes not. Falconer strode heedlessly along, as if daring anyone to empty a chamber pot on his head. No one did. One house had been boarded up, and a crude wooden cross nailed to its front door. Beneath the cross were scrawled the words LORD HAVE MERCY UPON US.

"Is that a church?" I said.

Falconer gave a derisive laugh. "That's a plague house, boy."

I shuddered. Though the plague had not been widespread in our parish, Dr. Bright had treated enough cases for me to know why that plea for mercy had been painted upon the door.

Ever since we left the inn, my stomach had been grow-ing distressed, and the stench that hung in the stagnant air of that street did nothing to improve it. I laid the blame on the fried fish and oysters I had eaten, but it might have been due to nervousness. Suddenly I was unsure that I was up to the task of copying a whole play. And if I failed, Fal-coner would not be pleased. I would have pleaded illness, but I knew that Falconer would brook no excuse short of my writing hand being lopped off—and even then he would probably insist that I transcribe left-handed.

At the end of the street, a set of narrow stone steps led to the water's edge. Falconer took them two at a time. I followed more cautiously and caught up just as he was handing several pennies to a waterman with a small wherry-boat.

"Get in," Falconer said.

"In the boat?" I had never imagined the theatre would lie across the river.

"No, in the water," he said acidly and, I hoped, sarcasti-cally.

It was no use protesting that I had never set foot in a boat in my life, and did not care to now, or that if the craft were to capsize I would be lost, for I had never learned to swim. There was nothing to do but to swallow my fear and step into the insubstantial bottom of the boat, which was all that lay between me and the Land of Rumbelow, that is to say a watery grave.

I took my place in the stern and sat gripping the gunwales with white-knuckled hands while Falconer climbed in, rocking the boat sickeningly, and the wherryman cast off.

Without the solid earth beneath my feet, my stomach grew even queasier. Before we were halfway across, I felt my dinner coming up. I tried to hold it back and, failing, thrust my head over the side of the boat and threw my fish back into the Thames, whence it had come. Unfortunately, I leaned out a bit too far. The boat listed suddenly, and I toppled over the side.

My head broke the surface of the water. But I had submerged only as far as my neck before something snatched the belt of my tunic and yanked me back aboard. It was Falconer. He set me forcibly in my seat and there I remained, sick and shamefaced, with water coursing from my hair, for the rest of the trip.

As we disembarked on the south bank, I said, "Thank you."

"For what?"

"For saving me life."

"I saved your master's investment, that's all." He headed down a wide road away from the river, and I trotted after.

"I'm sorry to have heaved up in the river."

Falconer snorted derisively. "There's enough garbage floating there already; a bit more will scarcely matter."

We were walking now in the company of a dozen or more theatregoers. The nearer we drew to the theatre, the more dense the crowd became. The people were of all positions and persuasions, from court ladies with coiffures that rivaled their skirts in volume to rank-smelling tanners' prentices. A number of the crowd turned down the lane that led to what I assumed was the theatre, but Falconer kept on straight ahead. "Is that not the theatre?"

"No. It's the bearbaiting."

I'd heard tell of bearbaitings but never witnessed one. Folk said it was a sport in which a bear, with its teeth broken off deliberately, was chained to a post and set upon by a pack of dogs. It did not sound very sporting to me.

A building that resembled an overgrown saltcellar lay ahead of us. I thought it circular at first, but it proved to be eight-sided, a good thirty feet in height, and three times that in breadth. I wondered that the ground here could support such a large structure. It was soft, swampy land, drained by half a dozen deep ditches, which we crossed on wooden footbridges.

The well-dressed patrons paid their admission to money gatherers, and mounted steps leading to upper galleries. The less elegant crowded through the main entrance and into a kind of courtyard. Above the entrance was a carving depicting Atlas with a globe of the world atop his shoulders—hence the theatre's name, the Globe. Under his feet was the legend *Totus mundus agit histrionem.*

I translated haltingly. "The whole world . . . practices theatrics?"

Falconer shook his head at my ignorance. "All the world's a stage. A line from *As You Like It.*"

"Oh," I said. "The play will not be in Latin, I trust?"

"No." Falconer made no move to approach the entrance but stood on the very fringes of the crowd, looking thoughtful. Finally he dug a penny from his purse and handed it to me. "Go on in."

"By *meself*?"

"Yes, yes, by yourself." He grasped my wrist and thrust the penny into my palm.

"But what an they—what an they catch me?"

"Whist!" Falconer held up a cautioning hand. "Softly!" In a low voice, he went on. "Just be certain they don't. And be certain you put down every word. Understood?"

"Aye," I said, forgetting in my anxiety the correct response.

"Go on, then!"

I felt in my wallet for the pad and pencil, then slipped into the stream of people which bore me, like a stick on the flood, through the entrance. A gatherer took my penny and I shuffled on, jostled from this side and that, until I bumped up against an unmoving mass of spectators. God help us, I thought, should the playhouse catch fire or collapse. We would all be trapped as surely as coneys in a snare.

The Globe's stage was a raised platform some ten yards across and equally as deep. Its boards were strewn with rushes. On the back wall were two curtained doorways, with a larger curtained space between them. Above these was a small balcony backed by a curtain and, above that, a thatched roof which covered the rear half of the stage.

A vendor with a basket of fruit and another selling leather bottles of beer wove through the crowd. The roar of voices and the smell of closely packed bodies were overpowering and unremitting. Even after a trumpeter appeared on a tiny balcony at the peak of the playhouse and blew a fanfare, the babble scarcely diminished. Nor did it leave off when two men in leather jerkins and helmets strode onto the stage.

At first, I thought they had been sent out to calm the crowd—or was it to apprehend would-be play pirates? I thrust my table-book and pencil into my wallet. As the chatter at last abated, the two men's words became audible, and I realized they were the players.

"Have you had a quiet guard?" one said, at the top of his voice.

"Not a mouse stirring," said the other, fairly shouting.

"Well, good night. If you do meet Horatio and Marcellus, the rivals of my watch, bid them make haste."

I fumbled frantically with the paper and pencil. Falconer had warned me to get down every word. Two more men entered, and I began to transcribe:

It was obvious at once that this would be no leisurely task, as copying those sermons back in Yorkshire had been. The players attacked their lines as though afraid that, if they did not keep their words in close order, the audience might throw comments of their own into the breach. And in fact, they often did.

My most pressing problem, however, was not the pell-mell flow of words, but how to identify each speaker on the page. All I could think of was to assign each a number, but that soon led to further confusion, as I forgot what number I'd given to which man. When half a dozen new players trooped out upon the stage, my heart sank into my shoes.

Gradually I learned the names of the major characters and labeled their lines accordingly. But then a new complication presented itself. I was caught up in the action of the play. I began to think of these people not as players mouthing speeches but as actual persons, living out a part of their lives before me.

Simon Bass had informed me that, because many considered the world of the theatre immoral, women were forbidden by law to act upon the stage. All women's roles were played by men and boys. That fact did not occur to me now. I was totally convinced that the Queen and Ophelia were what they seemed to be. In fact, Ophelia was quite fetching. So drawn in was I by the events on the stage that it seemed less important to me to copy down the lines than to find out what these people would say or do next.

When the ghost of Hamlet's father appeared upon the balcony and beckoned him, I gasped and shuddered but kept on writing. When Hamlet thrust his sword through the draperies, slaying Polonius, who was concealed there, I was lost. I no longer noticed the press of the crowd, nor its unwashed smell for I was no longer there among them, but in a castle in Denmark.

My petty mission no longer seemed to matter. All that mattered was whether or not Hamlet would take action to avenge his father. I wanted to call out to him, to tell him to stop delaying and debating, to go ahead and do what must be done. And yet I understood why he did not. I knew how it was to be swept along on the tide of events, and to feel you had no control over any of it, not even your own fate.

Every now and again, there was a passage of much talk and little action, and then I came to myself and began copying feverishly. But eventually I was drawn into the world of the play again, forgetting the world about me and the world outside, where Falconer waited.

From the onset of the fencing match between Hamlet and Laertes until Hamlet's death, I believe I did not commit to paper more than ten lines. I did get down every syllable of the final few speeches, but that was small comfort.

I had gone into the theatre fearful of being discovered and punished for writing down the play. I left with a dread of being punished for *not* having written it down. I need not have worried about the former; no one in the audience or on the stage had paid the least attention to my jottings.

Falconer, I knew, would not be so easy to fool. I hung back, trying to buy a little time in which to think. I could simply lie to Falconer, assure him that I'd transcribed the entire performance. Lying was one skill I'd acquired at the orphanage and polished during my apprenticeship to Dr. Bright. And of course there was no way Falconer could determine from looking at my scribbles whether or not I spoke the truth.

But eventually I was going to have to translate the play into ordinary script, and then the gaps would be as ostentatious as the slashes in the clothing of those young dandies I'd seen. To patch them in with a matching fabric would require an ability far greater than mine.

What to do, then? I would have to come up with some reasonable explanation very soon, for the theatre was rapidly emptying out. In a matter of minutes, I would be left standing in the arena all alone, like that toothless bear waiting to be savaged by the dogs.

8

The only thing I could think of to do was to admit that I'd overlooked a few lines, but lie about just how many, and hope that I'd be allowed a second chance. When I emerged on the tag end of the crowd, Falconer stood where I had left him, a dozen yards from the playhouse, his face turned toward the river, as though watching the slow progress of the coal barges. I considered bolting, losing myself in the crowd and thence in the streets of the city. But something made me hesitate. Perhaps it was the reward promised me by Simon Bass, perhaps it was the thought of having to fend for myself in this unfamiliar territory, perhaps it was both. Then Falconer turned and saw me, and it was too late. Gloomily, I approached him.

"Well?" he said.

"I got down most of it."

"*Most* of it?"

"Aye. Yes. The greater part. Nearly all, in fact. Save for a few wee bits here and there."

He smacked his fist into his palm so violently that I shrank back. "Why not all of it?"

"I—I couldn't hear well from where I stood. It was a very noisy crowd."

Falconer cursed under his breath. "How much is missing, exactly?"

"I don't ken, exactly."

"Twenty lines? Fifty? A hundred?"

I tried to choose a figure that would not sound too drastic yet would necessitate my coming back to fill in the gaps. "Not a hundred," I ventured. "Closer to fifty, I wis."

"You *wis*." He sighed heavily and stood watching the barges a moment. "When is the next performance of this play?"

"Friday, I wi—I think."

"Friday." Abruptly he turned to glare at me. "You'd best clean out your ears before then. Understood?"

"Aye. Yes. I will."

He stalked off, and I hastened after. As we neared the first of the footbridges, a man appeared from the rear of the playhouse and stepped onto the bridge. Falconer brushed past him so brusquely that he knocked the man off balance. The man stumbled sideways, tripped on the edge of the bridge, and splashed into the drainage ditch. He sprang up dripping wet, strode after Falconer, and snatched the back of Falconer's cloak, pulling the hood away from his head.

Falconer whirled about, his rapier already sweeping free of its hanger. The other man halted. His hand, too, went to his weapon. But before he could fully draw it, Falconer's sword point leaped forward. The move was so swift I am not certain I saw it clearly, but I believe he thrust his point through the guard of the other's weapon, then jerked upward. The man's rapier took flight and came to earth in the water of the ditch. With equal quickness, Falconer pulled the hood of his cloak forward again.

"Well," said the disarmed man, with surprising calm. "You have the advantage of me." Now that I heard his voice, I knew who he was—the first gravedigger in the play. Small wonder I did not recognize him at first; his appearance and speech were radically changed. Within the world of the play, he had been a shabby, half-drunk clown. Outside the playhouse walls, he cut quite a different figure. He was well built, well dressed, and well mannered, with nothing foolish or humble about him, despite the fact that he had just fallen into a ditch and been relieved of his weapon.

Falconer was putting away his sword. The player held up a hand to stay him. "Will you not allow me to salvage my weapon, sir, and with it my honor?"

Without replying, Falconer thrust his rapier into its hanger and turned away.

"May I at least know your name, then? One does not often meet a man with so disarming a manner."

I guessed that Falconer would not be able to resist a bit of wordplay, and I was right. "You know my arms. You need not know my name." It took me a moment to grasp the pun—if you recognized a man's coat of arms, then you knew his family name—but the player laughed appreciatively at once.

"It does seem to me that there is something familiar about you. Have we met before?"

"In another life, perhaps." Falconer strode away. The player gazed after him thoughtfully. I hastened after Falconer, not wishing to be left behind, but the player took hold of the sleeve of my tunic.

"What is your master's name?"

"Me master? Why, Dr. Bright," I said, perhaps out of old habit, perhaps as a deliberate lie—I was not sure which.

"*That* is Dr. Bright?" the player said incredulously, nodding after Falconer's departing figure.

"*That* is not me master. I don't ken that wight, and I'm as glad of it."

The man laughed. "He is an unmannerly lout, isn't he?" He let go of my sleeve. "You're merely a playgoer, then? Tell me, how did you like the play, a country lad like yourself?"

"Oh, very much," I said earnestly, trying not to seem anxious as Falconer faded from me.

"Did you indeed?" He stroked his short beard with a trace of amusement. "And what parts did you fancy most?"

"The fencing bout," I said instantly. "It looked so real!"

The man laughed. "Excellent!" He waded into the ditch and fished out his rapier. "I am the company's fencing master, you see." He looked ruefully at the muddy sword. "Though you would hardly guess it from that display just now."

"You are?" I was torn between catching up with Falconer and hearing more about the play.

"Aye." He climbed from the ditch and wiped his weapon in the grass.

I frowned. "You mock me speech."

"Not at all," he assured me. "I fell into it out of old habit. I'm a country wight meself, born and bred in Yorkshire. Judging from your speech, your master must be a South County man."

"Aye."

"But surely he's not the same Dr. Bright who authored the *Treatise on Melancholy*?"

"Aye. You don't mean you ken his work?"

"Oh, we do indeed ken it. In fact you might tell him that our Mr. Shakespeare has found his book invaluable. As you may have noticed, Hamlet is a very master of melancholy." He clapped me on the shoulder. "I'll be off now, or my colleagues will be several beers ahead of me, and I'll have trouble catching up." Laughing, he shook his head and licked his lips. "Performing works up a thirst like nothing else—save dueling, perhaps. Adieu, my young friend. Come see us again."

Unused to such civility, I let him get a dozen paces

down the road before I thought to reply. "Aye!" I called. "Thank you! I'll surely do that!"

After all, I thought, what choice did I have?

I found my way back to the bank of the Thames, but Falconer was nowhere in sight. Since I had no penny for passage—and did not care to risk my life in another boat, in any case—I would have to find another way of crossing the river. The only bridge was a formidable one of wood and stone several hundred yards downstream. In truth, it seemed less like a bridge than like a crowded city street, so heavily laden with shops that I feared the whole affair might collapse under the rumbling wheels of the carts and the pounding hooves of the horses.

Once safely on the north bank, I asked a cheerful fish-wife the way to The George, where I found Falconer eating his supper—fish, again.

"So, you finally found your way," he said.

"The player—'a held me back."

"And what did you tell him?"

"Naught. Just as you said I should."

He stared at me a long moment with his shadowed eyes, as if trying to see into my soul. Then he devoured the last of his meal and rose. "I don't like liars," he said, his voice low and harsh. "I hope you are not one."

I shook my head emphatically, too intimidated to speak. I don't believe he noticed, for he was already on his way upstairs.

9

I saw little of Falconer over the next two days. Around midday on Friday, he came to the stable where, to pass the time, I was helping the stableboy curry horses. He neither spoke nor beckoned to me, only stepped back out into the courtyard, knowing I would follow.

He was even less talkative than usual, but finally, as we walked down a deserted alley, he said, "Be sure you complete your work today. We've lost our lodgings."

"Lost them?"

"I killed one of the other lodgers. In a duel."

It was several minutes before I recovered from this news enough to ask, "What—what was it about, then? The duel?"

I was certain he would reprimand me for talking too

much. But he did not. Instead he replied, "The man called me a filthy Jew."

Something possessed me to ask, "Are you?"

"Filthy? Or a Jew?" He sounded almost amused.

"A Jew."

He gave a short, bitter laugh. "There are no Jews in England. Only former Jews."

The sky scowled down upon us, threatening rain as we boated over to Southwark and joined the throng of bear-baiters and playgoers. At the Globe, Falconer drew me aside. "We must find a better vantage point for you, one where you will hear *every* word."

"The galleries?" I suggested.

"Among those overdressed fops and their painted doxys? You might as well go right up on stage. No, I've a better spot for you. Come." He led me to the rear of the playhouse, to the players' entrance. The door stood ajar, and through the crack, I could just make out lines being spoken on the stage.

"This is no better," I whispered.

"Not here. Up there." He pointed to the stairs beside us. "Through that door. Conceal yourself behind the curtains at the rear of the small balcony."

I gaped upward. "Up *there*? But—"

His hand closed painfully around my upper arm. "And mark me! No excuses this time. I want every word set down. Understood?"

Wincing, I nodded. His grip relaxed, and he pushed me roughly toward the stairs. "Go on, then."

I reluctantly mounted the stairs, wondering how it was that Falconer knew this playhouse so intimately. I cracked the door, listened a moment, then peered in. The interior was dim and deserted. Apparently the ghost had already done his turn on the balcony and departed. I slipped through the entrance and pulled the door carefully closed. From that spot, I could hear clearly every word spoken by Hamlet, for his voice carried well. But the speeches of the less forceful players were still lost.

I tiptoed to the draperies that hung at the rear of the balcony. When I pulled back the edge of the drape slightly, I could hear well enough; I could also see the front half of the stage. Hamlet stood there, conversing with the ghost of his father. The ghost's hollow, haunting voice—a voice not unlike Falconer's—sent a shiver up my spine.

I clenched my teeth resolutely, determined not to be caught up in the play again, and set to work transcribing all that had slipped by me before. Now that I knew how the story came out, I could concentrate better on my task. But I was still nervous about being discovered, and jumped at every sound.

Halfway through the performance, my writing hand grew cramped, but otherwise there were no problems. I believe I still lost a line or two during the riveting fencing match, but no one would miss them. As the end neared, I congratulated myself silently—and, as it turned out, prematurely.

At Hamlet's death, my work was done; I had copied the rest on my previous visit. Greatly relieved and, at the same time, a little sorry because I might never have a chance to see a play again, I closed the table-book and backed away, meaning to slip out as quietly as I had come in.

It was then that I heard footfalls on the stairs—not the outside steps I had used, but a steep, narrow flight rising from behind the stage. I choked back a gasp and desperately glanced about for a place of concealment. Seeing none, I ducked between the end of the drapery and the wall. There was just enough room for me to stand there without being seen by the audience, provided I did not move so much as a finger.

The footsteps drew near. The drapes parted in the center, and a man in soldier's garb stepped onto the balcony, where a small cannon stood bolted to the floor. He dumped a charge of powder down the bore of the cannon, rammed in a wad of cloth, and set a fuse in the fuse-hole. As he lifted his smouldering stick of touchwood and blew on it, he caught sight of me for the first time.

His eyes widened. He took a step toward me, then hesitated and glanced back at the cannon, obviously torn between apprehending me and being faithful to his cue. I started to slip away, but to my dismay, the point of the dagger in my belt snagged on the edge of the drape.

I fought desperately with the fabric, struggling to free myself. The audience had now spotted me and were tittering and pointing. As the cannoneer started for me again, his cue was spoken on the stage: "Go, bid the soldiers shoot."

Glaring at me, he rushed to the cannon, knocking it askew in his haste, and thrust the touchwood against the fuse. Nothing happened. Furious, he blew on the wood and touched the fuse again. The cannon went off, a full thirty seconds late, and the man descended on me.

I gave the drapery a prodigious yank and was free. As I stumbled for the door, the cannoneer burst through the center of the curtain and blocked my path. I looked about frantically. The only other route of escape was the inside stairs. I scrambled for them and, clinging to the rickety railing, half-ran, half-fell down them, with the soldier hard upon my heels.

I was not quite halfway to the bottom when the burly, greybearded man who had played the second gravedigger suddenly appeared at the foot of the stairs. I was trapped.

My only chance for escape lay in jumping off the stairs to the floor below, a fall of some six or eight feet—risky, but better to sprain an ankle than to be whipped or put in the stocks. I ducked under the railing and was about to leap when a cry rang through the theatre that stopped every one of us dead in his tracks. "Fire! Fire!"

The stocky greybeard at the foot of the stairs shook a finger at me, as if to say he'd deal with me later, then hastened away. The cannoneer came thundering down the steps, but I scrambled faster than he and ran for the rear door. When I burst through it, Falconer was gone. I ran on, around the side of the playhouse.

People were streaming out of the main entrance in panic. The elegant ladies from the gallery scurried fearfully down the steps, hoisting their vast skirts above their ankles in an unseemly way. One was sobbing, and the tears made tracks through her heavy white makeup.

I was mostly afraid of being pursued. I pushed into the center of the noisy, milling mob. Some were staring at the roof of the theatre. When I followed their gaze, I saw a thick cloud of grey smoke rising from the thatch, to become lost in the darker grey of the sky.

The players had set a ladder on the uppermost landing of the outside stairs, and several of them were now on the roof, beating at the smouldering thatch with their capes. A line of men, comprised of players and audience alike, formed between the playhouse and the nearest drainage ditch. They dipped up buckets of water and passed them from hand to hand along the line, up the stairs and the ladder to the men on the roof, who tossed the water onto the spreading flames.

In the middle of the line, passing buckets with the rest, stood the slim boy who had played Ophelia. He was wigless now but still in his stage makeup. Above the waist, he wore the bodice of his lady-like costume; below it, he wore men's breeches and hose.

"What set it off?" said a man next to me.

"The wad from the cannon, is my guess," said another.

My stomach twisted. If that was so, then I was partly to blame, for I had distracted the cannoneer and caused him to misdirect the shot. I had seen buildings burn before. In fact, it was not uncommon, even in a village as small as Berwick. But I had never before been the cause. Furthermore, I felt as though it were something more than a mere building at stake. It was an entire world, one into which I had been privileged to look briefly, and which was now in danger of crumbling.

So distressed was I that I was on the verge of lending my efforts to the fire fighters, even at the risk of being recognized. Then someone jostled me from behind, bringing me to my senses. I whirled about, expecting to see Falconer at my elbow, demanding the completed script. But it was only a thin fellow with a red nose and a scraggly beard, smiling apologetically. "Begging your pardon, my young friend," he said and moved off through the crowd.

Now that my thoughts were on Falconer, I cast my eyes about for him, but my stature was so small and the throng so dense that I stood no hope of spotting him. I turned back to the drama being played out atop the theatre.

The men on the roof were making little headway against the flames. They would, I believe, have lost their livelihood had not the gloomy sky chosen that moment to open up, dousing the burning thatch with more water than the poor players could have carried to it in a week. A cheer went up from the line of water bearers, then from the crowd. I joined in.

I was so relieved that I scarcely minded the soaking rain. I turned my face up to it and laughed appreciatively. The timing of the deluge had been so perfect, I could almost believe it was some grand theatrical effect produced by the company for our amazement. The whole world practices theatrics, I thought, and laughed again.

Then, as the crowd dispersed, I caught a glimpse of a sinister figure standing at a distance, looking out over the river as before. Sighing, I moved toward him. I laid one hand on my wallet, to reassure myself that the hard-won script was still safely tucked within. The pouch seemed flat and empty. My heart suddenly felt the same. I halted, yanked up the flap of the wallet, and plunged my hand inside. My fingers closed on the pencil, but the table-book was unquestionably, inexplicably gone.

For a moment, I stood unmoving and unthinking, feeling as though I'd been struck soundly on the brain-pan. Then my mind began to react. How could the table-book be gone? I clearly remembered putting it in my wallet back on the balcony of the theatre. I turned the wallet upside down and shook it vigorously, as if hoping the book was lodged in some out-of-the-way corner. It was not, of course.

I glanced fearfully at Falconer. He was still gazing out over the Thames. Cautiously, I backed toward the play-house. When I had put several groups of lingering theatre-goers between him and me, I retraced the course I had taken when I emerged so hastily from the playhouse a short time before. I wiped the rain from my eyes and scanned every inch of the soggy ground. If I didn't find the table-book soon, it would be a useless mass of pulp.

But already I was halfway around the building and had seen nothing but orange peels and apple cores, discarded playbills and ballad-sheets. To proceed was to risk encountering the men from whom I'd just escaped. Yet, if it came down to it, I might be better off with them than facing Falconer without the script in my hands. After all, he had killed a man just for calling him a Jew. Though I doubted my fate would be so drastic, the man was unpredictable. Even if all he did was abandon me, that in itself was a frightening prospect. How would I survive in this strange city on my own?

I went on, keeping my eyes open both for the table-book and for trouble. I came to within a few yards of the rear door and still saw no sign of either. "The devil take me," I breathed. "It must be inside, then."

It took me some time to muster the nerve required to pull the door open an inch or two and peer inside. Just as I stuck my face up to the crack, the door flew open, knocking me on the forehead and sending me flying backward, to land on my huckle bones in the mud.

Before I could scramble away, a strong hand took my arm and pulled me to my feet. "Well, now," a hearty voice said. "What have we here?"

Groaning, I held my hand to my afflicted head and squinted at my captor. It was the second gravedigger, the hefty old man who had blocked my way on the stair. "You've brast me costard!" I complained.

He laughed at my Upland speech. "Brast your costard, have I? Well, it serves you right, for all your mischief. What are you up to, scuttling about behind the stage like a great rat?"

"Me?" I tried to sound as innocent as I might while moaning in pain. "Behind the stage?"

The old man laughed again. "Ho, quite the actor, aren't you? Perhaps you belong *on* the stage and not behind it, eh? Yes, my lad, you're the only one going about in a pudding-basin hair style and a skirt, I'm afraid." He referred to my knee-length tunic and the bowl-shaped haircut common among country lads. He gently pulled my hand away from my head. "Hmm. That is a nasty bump you've suffered, though. Come. No use getting drenched into the bargain." Keeping a firm hold on my arm, he led me inside.

I considered breaking free and making a run for it. He was, after all, an old man, and I, though slow to sprout, was fleet of foot. But he was also a brawny man, and his grip was as inescapable as Falconer's. My brain, which had always been as fleet as my feet, began to race instead, looking for a way out. What was it the man had said—that I belonged on the stage rather than behind it? Perhaps my salvation lay that way.

The old player ushered me through the cluttered area behind the stage and into a large, windowed room where most of the company stood or sat about in various stages of undress. Several were grimy with soot from the fire, and one man had a large part of his beard singed away. All were rain soaked. Yet they did not appear miserable in the least; instead, they were laughing and joking, as though they had just played a game of bowls and not fought a potentially disastrous fire.

The cannoneer, who was cleaning mud from his costume, was the first to notice our entrance. "So!" he called, over the uproar. "You've caught the dirty dastard, Mr. Pope!"

My captor set me down on a stool. "Yes, he made the classic mistake of all criminals; he returned to the scene of the crime."

I tried to rise, but he pushed me down. "I'm no criminal!" I protested, wondering if someone had come across my lost table-book.

A tall, kindly looking man who had been Polonius in the play said, "Of c-course you're not." I did not recall him stuttering on stage, but he did so now. He bent and looked closely at my bruised forehead. "Wh-what did you hit him with, T-Thomas? Your sh-shovel?"

My captor, whose name, I gathered, was Thomas Pope, looked hurt. "I am not a violent man. The fact is, I opened a door into his head."

"A d-door into his head, eh? I hope his b-brains didn't spill out."

"I'll spill his brains," the cannoneer threatened. "This is the hoddypeak who caused me to miss my aim, Mr. Heminges, and shoot that wad into the thatch."

"I hardly think he is to b-blame for that," Mr. Heminges said. "However, it is t-true that you disrupted our performance. Would you c-care to explain why?"

Though the throbbing in my head had subsided, I went on holding it and grimacing pitifully but bravely, to play on their sympathies. "I meant no harm. I only wished to see the play."

"The usual method," Mr. Pope said, "is to pay your penny and stand in *front* of the stage."

"I ken that. But I ha' no penny."

Mr. Pope clucked his tongue incredulously. "What sort of master would refuse his prentice a penny to see a play?"

"Well, the truth is . . . I ha' no master."

"You've c-come to London on your own?" said Mr. Heminges.

"Aye."

"For what purpose?"

It was time to bring into play the strategy that had been forming in my mind. But not too quickly. "You'll laugh at me."

"Not I," Mr. Heminges assured me.

Hesitantly, I said, "I want . . . I want to be a player."

True to his word, Mr. Heminges did not laugh—but several of the others did, and he gave them an exasperated glance. "You t-truly believe you would want to t-turn Turk and become like these disreputable wights?"

"Aye, by these bones, I would," I lied earnestly. In truth, aside from wanting to escape a beating, or wanting a meal, I had scarcely ever given any thought to what I wanted. No one had ever asked.

"Ahh, he's as full of lies as an egg is of meat," Jack, the cannoneer, said.

"I believe him," a voice beside me said. It was the first gravedigger, the man who had crossed swords so briefly with Falconer a few days before. "Though you did lie about not having a master," he reprimanded me. "You told me Dr. Bright was your master. Come, the truth now. You've run off, haven't you?"

I hung my head in mock remorse. "Aye."

"There, now," said the cannoneer. "If he lied about that, how do you know he's telling the truth about wanting to be a player?"

"Well," the other man said, "for one thing, he's seen the play before, and talked to me with some enthusiasm about it. Why risk a thrashing in order to see it a second time? And why desert his master and come to London alone unless he has a strong hunger for some food to be found nowhere else?" He looked about at the other players. "You've felt that hunger, every mother's son of you. Would you refuse to let him satisfy it?"

Mr. Heminges scratched his beard thoughtfully. "As

f-far as that g-goes, we could use another b-boy. Nick's golden voice threatens to turn b-bass any day now, and his b-beard to betray him." There was general merriment over this, and the strapping boy who had played the queen flushed and kicked the shin of the laughing youth next to him.

"This is a democratic c-company. Let us p-put the matter to a vote. All who favor t-taking on—What is your name, my young friend?"

With no time to concoct a lie, I said, "Widge."

Mr. Heminges's eyebrows raised skeptically. "All who favor taking on *W-Widge* as our new p-prentice." Most of the hands in the room went up. The cannoneer and the boy named Nick were the sole objectors. "That settles it. Widge, allow me to w-welcome you to the Lord Chamberlain's c-company."

11

Though I had been transported by the magic of these players, I had no thought in the world that I could become one of them. I thought only of doing what I had been hired to do. I meant to retrieve my table-book or, failing that, to seek an opportunity to transcribe the play again. Better yet, I might manage to make off with the theatre's copy, saving myself a good deal of toil and trouble.

"Now," Mr. Heminges said. "Who would like to b-be responsible for this b-boy?"

Mr. Pope clapped a heavy hand on my shoulder. "I suppose I can make room for one more. He's not very large. You don't eat much, do you, lad?"

"I hardly ken, sir. I've never had the chance to find out." This, said in all seriousness, earned me a laugh from the players. I had been laughed at for being a fool, but never for being witty. I found it pleased me.

"Well answered," Mr. Pope said. "Come then. Goodwife Willingson will be waiting supper for us." As he ushered me through the door, he called over his shoulder, "Sander!"

"Coming!" a voice from the far side of the room replied. As we passed behind the stage, I glanced furtively about for the incriminating table-book. The boy Mr. Pope had called Sander caught up with us just outside the rear door. He was of an age with me, but nearly a head taller, and as thin as Banbury cheese.

"Widge," said Mr. Pope, "shake hands with Alexander Cooke, known familiarly as Sander."

The boy pumped my hand as though he expected me to spout water. "Welcome to the company, Widge. It's a lot of work, but it's fun as well."

Work? I thought. What could be so difficult about dressing up in fine clothing and saying witty and poetic things already written out for you?

The rain had dwindled to a fine drizzle—what we in Yorkshire called a cobweb day. We were soaked by the time we reached Mr. Pope's home, though it lay a mere five minutes' walk from the Globe. All the way there, I cast my eyes about furtively, wondering if Falconer would return to find me.

"Sander," said Mr. Pope, "see if you can hunt up a change of clothing for Widge. He looks as though he's been wrestling pigs."

Sander led me upstairs to a small dormer room. The walls were papered with hundreds of broadsides and ballad-sheets, plus playbills for half a dozen theatres. While I looked them over, Sander rummaged through an ironbound chest and tossed me a short kersey tunic and a pair of plain breeches. "Try those. I've grown out of them."

As we changed, I glanced about the room. "You ha' this all to yourself?"

"Until now."

"Oh. I'm sorry."

He shrugged. "I don't mind. It'll give me somebody to talk to—and to study lines with."

"They let you perform in the plays?"

"Sometimes. Not the one today. Usually I play a serving maid or some such."

"So you ha' no copy of *Hamlet*?"

Sander laughed. "No one gets a copy of the whole play."

"But then how do you con your speeches?"

"Learn the lines, you mean? Oh, you get a little sheaf of paper we call a *side*, with just your part on it. You'll see."

"But there has to be a copy of the whole play somewhere," I insisted.

"Of course. The book keeper keeps it under lock and key. People filch them sometimes, you know. Do their own version. It hurts our box, then."

"Box. That's the money you take in," I said, recalling Simon Bass's words.

"Right. But the worst of it is, they don't give Mr. Shakespeare a farthing for it. And it is his work, after all." He gave my new attire a critical glance. "That looks well enough. A bit loose, but clean and dry at least. Let's go now, or we'll have Goody Willingson angry with us. She's the housekeeper."

"Does she beat you, then?" I asked softly as we descended the stairs.

Sander laughed. "Mistress Willingson? She can hardly bear to beat the carpets."

"And Mr. Pope? Does he beat you?"

Sander turned to me with a puzzled look. "Say, what sort of family are you used to?"

"Family?" I said.

Mr. Pope was already at the table, along with half a dozen young boys who, I later learned, were orphans Mr. Pope had taken in. The housekeeper showed no sign of exasperation at our lateness. She merely filled plates and set them before us.

The other boys were well behaved, except for staring at me, the newcomer. I kept my attention on my plate and tried to ignore them.

"So," Mr. Pope said. "You've run off from your master."

I choked down a piece of beef. "Aye."

"Will he be content to let you go, or will he come after you?"

"I can't say." In truth, I was certain that, should I really desert, Simon Bass would not let me go lightly. He was a man of business, and I suspected he would not like losing the ten pounds sterling he had invested in me. To such a man, I would not be a runaway prentice but an uncollected debt. And Falconer would be the collector.

"Well, I can sympathize with you," Mr. Pope was saying. "I was apprenticed to a weaver myself, before I heard the theatre's siren call. Most of the members of our company, in fact, were destined for some more respectable trade. Mr. Heminges was to be a goldsmith, Mr. Shakespeare a glover." He looked sternly about at the young children. "That is not to say that I condone prentices running off willy-nilly from their masters. You will all be prentices one day, and I expect each of you to work hard at learning your trade—just as I expect Widge, here, to work hard at becoming a player." He turned his gaze on me again. I gave what I hoped would pass for an eager look and turned my attention to my plate once more.

How had I gotten myself into this? Until today, there had been but one set of demands upon me. Now two threats hung over me, like the buildings in that narrow, stinking alley. Sooner or later, they were sure to meet, and I would be caught squarely in the middle, up to my ears in muck-water.

The bed I shared with Sander was the softest I had known, and Sander neither tossed nor snored unduly. Yet I slept fitfully. Once I even rose and began to dress, thinking that the most prudent course might be to run away. But I could not think of anywhere to run. I crept back into bed and lay there, contemplating the terrible sorts of fates that seem possible only in the small hours, until matins rang.

Though it was not fully light, Sander and I dressed, breakfasted, and set out for the Globe. I glanced into each alley we passed, half expecting to spy a cloaked figure waiting to spring on me. But of course Falconer had no way of knowing where I was, and I didn't think he would haunt the vicinity of the theatre; for some reason he had seemed reluctant to show himself there. Probably he feared that someone would guess his purpose. One thing I was sure of—he was still in London somewhere and still determined to have the script. The thought made me newly determined to have it as a shield against his wrath when he caught up with me, as he surely would.

We were far from the first arrivals at the playhouse. Men were busy re-thatching the roof. Behind the stage, others were carrying pieces of scenery and furniture upstairs, and carrying new ones down.

Gone was any hope I had harbored of searching for my table-book. Players stood or sat in odd corners, talking to themselves, making curious faces and sudden gestures, for all the world like residents of a madhouse.

A ruddy-faced young man gave an unexpected sweep of his arm, striking me on the side of the head. I backed away, ready to apologize for getting in the way. To my surprise, the man was the one to offer an apology. "Sorry. Didn't see you."

He turned to Sander, waving his script. "Mr. Jonson has

kindly provided me with thirty new lines to learn before today's performance. I had difficulty enough recalling the old ones."

Sander patted him on the shoulder. "You'll learn them, Will. You always do. And if you don't, you'll make something up." In a confidential voice, he added, "Something better, no doubt."

The man named Will gave a grudging smile. "I suppose so."

"So, the performance is on for today? I thought it looked like rain again."

"You know how they are." Will rolled his eyes upward, as though referring to the gods, but I presumed he meant the men who held shares in the company. "We'll go on unless the stage is under water, and even then they'd likely haul out boats and do *The Spanish Armada*."

Sander laughed. "They'll be wanting the stage cleared, then. I'll tell you what; I'll learn your lines for you if you'll clear the stage for me."

Will waved him away. Sander picked up two brooms and handed one to me. I glanced back at Will, who was mumbling and gesturing again. "Surely that was not Mr. Shakespeare?"

Sander gave a laugh that held no disdain, only amusement. "Hardly. That's Will Sly. He was a prentice like us a few years ago. Now he's a hired man. You won't see much of Mr. Shakespeare. He's a private man, and a very busy one. But no—you have seen him."

"I have?"

"He was the ghost in *Hamlet*." He pulled back the curtain and let me precede him onto the stage. Bereft of players and properties, it bore no resemblance to a castle in Denmark. It was a mere platform of boards, covered with damp and dirty rushes.

On the ground, two boys of about nine or ten years of age were gathering discarded beer bottles and mashed fruit. "Samuel and James," Sander told me. "Our hopefuls."

"Hopeful of what?"

"Of staying on as prentices." He rolled up his sleeves. "Well, let's have at it."

We spent the next hour sweeping the heavy mat of soiled and soggy rushes onto the ground, spreading a fresh supply from a wagon over the boards, then loading the old ones on the wagon. By the time we finished, I was as limp and wet as the rushes. I sank down on the edge of the stage. "No one told me a player's life would be like this."

Sander gave another good-humored laugh. How could he be so cheerful in the face of such drudgery? "We don't do this every day. Some days we clean out the jakes and pile it on the dung heap."

I shook my head wearily and silently prayed that I might find the missing table-book very soon. "When does a wight get to be a hired man?"

"When your voice changes. If you're a good prentice, meantime." Sander picked up his broom. "Come. Time for lessons."

"I already ken how to read and write," I pointed out as we climbed the narrow stairs I had scrambled down the day before. Even as I spoke, my eyes were casting about for some sign of my table-book.

"That will be useful," Sander said, "but these are lessons of a different sort."

Behind us as we came up the stairs was a large room in which a group of players were rehearsing some scene. We proceeded past the drapes on which I had snagged myself; I saw no table-book there, either. I would have to return later and search more carefully.

We stopped outside the door to another room. From within the room came the sound of blows, and an occasional cry. I felt a wrenching in my stomach. Whatever lessons lay ahead, they were obviously being driven home with the aid of a willow switch. First hard labor, now beatings. I should have known the theatre would prove to be as heartless and harsh as any other institution.

I hung back, very nearly resolved to flee and take my chances with Falconer—had I known where he was—or even on my own in that unknown city.

But just then Sander turned and beckoned to me with such a cheerful and friendly countenance that I swallowed my misgivings and followed him inside the lesson room.

The scene within was not at all what I had expected. There were no sullen students lined up on benches with slates in their hands. Nor was there any sign of anyone being beaten. The sounds had apparently come from two boys mock sword fighting with wooden singlesticks. One was Nick, the fellow who had been the butt of the players' jokes the day before, and who had played the queen in *Hamlet*. The other was the play's Ophelia, a slender boy no taller than I, and far better suited to playing girls' parts than the swaggering Nick, who seemed too husky in voice and in build to portray anything but older women.

On the other side of the room, two players were dancing a jig to a tune played on an hautboy. Nearby, Samuel and James, the two hopefuls, were turning somersets atop a row of rush mats, under the eye of a small, athletic-looking man.

"Mr. Phillips," Sander informed me. "He's our stage manager, among other things. Mr. Armin you already know." He gestured toward the man who had run afoul of Falconer, and who had stood up for me before the other players. He was demonstrating sword positions to Nick and his partner. He nodded in our direction, and Sander approached him. "Where shall I start our new boy?"

"Stramazone!" Mr. Armin shouted, and I shrank back, believing we were being cursed in some foreign tongue. The two students made slicing motions with their sticks. "He may as well begin here," Mr. Armin said, in a perfectly civil tone. Then he shouted, *"Riversa!"* The two boys cut with their sticks from the other side. "Get him a single-stick."

For the next hour I stood in a rank with Sander and the others, facing Mr. Armin and attempting to duplicate his stance and movements. I had never had anything to do with weapons, beyond the mock skirmishes with elder sticks at the orphanage. Before long, my limbs began to ache. I could sense that the others were secretly laughing at my bumbling efforts, and I longed to throw the stick aside—preferably at them—and show them my skill with a pen. But to do so, of course, would be to give myself away.

I would have to continue to seem a willing prentice until I could complete my real mission here. And when I did, when I had stolen the script from under their very noses, then I would be the one to laugh.

At last Mr. Armin called a halt, and he and Nick paired off. Nick was armed with a real rapier, now—blunted, of course. They saluted with their swords, their faces smiling and cordial. Then Mr. Armin said "Have at you!" and the two transformed before our eyes into deadly enemies. Their blades clashed and parted and met again with such rapidity that my eye could scarcely follow.

Sander and Ophelia cheered them on. Their sentiments were obviously with Mr. Armin, but they shouted encouragement to Nick as well. Even with my ignorance of fencing, I could see that Mr. Armin was holding back, giving Nick time to ward and counter. The fencing scene in the play had displayed this same measured pace. As with the play, I was drawn into the drama. Just as I was tempted to shout a word of encouragement myself, Mr. Armin effortlessly caught Nick's sideways blow on the guard of his rapier, flung his arm outward, and delivered a quick but gentle *stocatta* to Nick's unguarded chest. "Touch," he said.

Nick's face, already red from exertion, grew redder. He peevishly flung down the rapier and stalked off. Mr. Armin ignored his outburst and approached us. "Do you three feel you're ready for a real weapon?"

"No, sir!" we said, almost as one person.

"Then go practice your *passatas*," he said. "We have an audience who pays to see us; we don't need you lot standing about gawking."

As we moved away, Sander said, "Widge is going to need a bit of coaching, I think. Do you want to do it, Julian, or shall I?"

Ophelia, whose name was apparently Julian, shrugged. "We could take turns."

"All right with you, Widge?" Sander asked.

Unused as I was to being asked my preferences, I took a moment to reply. "Oh, aye. I don't mind. But Mr. Armin said—"

"Fie on what Mr. Armin said," Sander replied, but softly. "I've done so many *passatas* I could do them in my sleep."

"Just be sure you do them on your side of the bed."

He laughed. "We'll soon have you doing them in your sleep as well. Now, the first thing we'll have to show you is the three wards."

"Three words?"

"No, wards." He held the singlestick at the height of his forehead. "This is high ward." I copied his stance. He moved the stick to his waist. "Broad ward." His hand went down near his knee. "Base ward."

"You might just as well show him the right way,

Cooke," a voice said. I turned to see Nick standing close by. "Here, let me have that stick." Sander gave it up reluctantly. Nick planted himself in front of me, a distinctly unpleasant smile on his face. "I'll learn you properly."

"Let him be," Sander said, not as forcefully as he might have.

"I'm only going to see that he learns his lesson," Nick said innocently. "Now then. Widge, is it? You know what a widge is where I come from?"

My throat felt too tight to speak. I shook my head.

"A horse. I think I'll call you Horse, though you look more like an ass to me. Hold your stick like this, Horse—the hand close to the knee, and the tip pointing at your opponent's throat-bole."

With a shaking hand, I tried to mirror his position.

"Get your point up," he commanded. I was slow to respond, and he whacked my stick sharply. "Get the point up, I said. Get the point?"

"Aye."

"Aye? Do I look like the captain of a ship?"

"Nay."

"Ah, you can neigh like a horse as well. Now, bring your hoof—I mean your *hand*—in closer to your leg, else your opponent might do *this*." He brought his stick swiftly down on my knuckles. With a gasp, I let my stick fall. "And if you do that, he'll certainly do *this*." He lunged, and his stick struck my breastbone painfully.

My fear gave way to anger, and I scrambled for the

fallen weapon. Laughing, Nick knocked it out of my reach. When I was young at the orphanage, and the bigger boys taunted me, I invariably burst into tears. But finding that it was an invitation to further abuse, I had learned to refrain from tears, whatever the provocation. I even prided myself on it. Now, facing Nick, I trembled with shame and frustration, but I was dry-eyed.

"Pick it up, Horse," Nick ordered me. With his foot, he sent it skating across the floor at me.

As I hesitated, unsure whether I would look more like a fool by picking it up or by letting it lie, Julian suddenly stepped between us, his stick at broad ward. "That's enough, Nick. We can all see he's no match for you."

"And you are, I suppose."

"No," the boy replied evenly. "But Sander and I together may be."

Nick scowled at Sander, who had taken the cue and come up behind him. "That's unfair odds."

"So is you against Widge," Sander said. "Give him a few months of practice, and he'll go a round with you, won't you, Widge?"

Though in truth I meant to be gone long before that, I nodded. "Aye."

Nick pointed his stick threateningly at me. "Study your footwork well, then, Hobbyhorse, for I mean to hobble you." He gave a token thrust toward Sander, who jumped back. Laughing, Nick tossed the stick aside and swaggered off.

Only then did I notice Mr. Armin watching from across the room. "Why did 'a not put a stop to 't?"

"I suppose," Julian said, "he believes a man should fight his own battles."

"Then why did you step in?" I said crossly.

"I beg your humble pardon! Next time I'll let him put a dent in your stupid pudding basin!" Julian stomped away.

"A bit of a hothead, isn't 'a?" I observed.

"And you're a bit of a muttonhead," Sander said mildly. "He was only trying to help."

"I don't need any help," I said sullenly.

"Yes, you do. Now why don't you take up that stick, and we'll start over. High ward." As I grudgingly strove to mimic his movements, he said, "Nick isn't really such a bad sort, you know. He was just testing your mettle. Broad ward. I don't think Nick is truly mean at heart. He's just going through a bad time. He's been a prentice for six or seven years, and now he'll have to begin playing a man's part."

"On the stage, or in life?"

"Both, I suppose. Low ward."

"That's as may be," I said. "But we can scarcely judge a person by what 'a's like inside. It's th' outside we ha' to do wi'."

Sander lowered his singlestick and sighed. "Well, on the inside you may be a very good fencer, but on the outside you stink."

"I washed but last week," I protested.

Sander laughed. "I didn't mean it literally, you goose. It means you're terrible. Come. We'll try some *passatas*."

It was a long morning. When Mr. Armin finally tired of trying to make us into some semblance of "scrimers"—his word for swordsmen—he passed us on to Mr. Phillips, who worked on our diction—mostly mine—and something called projection, which meant, as nearly as I could tell, shouting more loudly than the audience.

To my relief, the afternoon was less taxing. The company was presenting a play called *Every Man Out of His Humour*, which fit my mood exactly. As the book keeper was ill, Sander was given the task of holding the play book and throwing out lines to players who were floundering.

I was posted, along with Samuel, one of the hopefuls, in the tiring-room to help the players change costume. In my ignorance, I did more to hinder than to help, yet none complained—except Nick. When I stepped on the hem of his gown, he aimed a blow at me. I ducked it easily; ducking was one athletic skill I had long since mastered. Before he could try it again, his cue came. "I'll see to you later, Horse," he growled, and swept out. His voice was so much at odds with his feminine appearance that I could not help snickering.

"Such a lady," Sam said, and set us both laughing.

Julian came into the tiring-room, greeted us, and retreated into the wardrobe to change. I stared after him. "Feels 'a's too good for us, does 'a?"

"Oh, it's nothing against us," Sam said. "He's a modest

one, is all. Mr. Shakespeare's the same, and Mr. Burbage. Don't like others pawing them, I guess."

The mention of Mr. Shakespeare brought to mind something that the day's constant activity had pushed aside—the lost script. If I did not find it soon, someone else would. Leaving Sam to take care of matters in the tiring-room, I crept up the stairs to the balcony.

My luck was good that day; the balcony was not in use. I drew back the drapery and inspected the spot where I'd concealed myself the day before.

So much for luck. The notebook was not there. Where in heaven's name was it, then? Had some member of the company found it?

Then it came to me: the man in the crowd who had jostled me from behind. He had smiled so sincerely. It never occurred to me that he had dipped his thieving fingers in my wallet. "Gog's bread!" I murmured. "'A's stolen me script!"

The thief must have been upset to discover that he had filched not a purse but a book full of scribbles. He could hardly return it, though. And however great his frustration, it could not have held a candle to the dismay that I felt at that moment, knowing that all my work and worry was for naught.

Despite my exhaustion, I lay awake a long time that night, wondering how I could possibly survive another week of lessons until such time as *Hamlet* came around again. And how would I manage to transcribe it unobserved? I tried hard to think of some alternative.

Perhaps I could copy out the players' individual parts from their "sides." The problem with that was that they had all learned their parts and seldom used the sides. What about the book used to prompt the players, then? But I had seen how diligently Sander guarded it, never letting it out of his hands, let alone his sight. At last my battered brain succumbed to sleep.

The following day, Sunday, the theatre was closed. I was grateful for the day off, and for the chance to sleep late. In truth, I slept only an hour or so past matins; then several of Mr. Pope's orphans invaded our room, begging for stories and horseback rides.

At first I refused. Bad enough to be called Horse by Nick; now I was expected to behave as one. But when the boys pleaded with me, tugging eagerly at my sleeve, it brought to my mind a picture of myself at that age, tugging at Mistress MacGregor's skirts as she handed out the contents of some charity basket. Grudgingly I let myself be pulled down onto all fours, straddled, and spurred by bare feet into a sluggish gait.

Sander, burdened with a pair of riders, glanced at me and grinned broadly. I shook my head in exasperation. "Make horsie noises!" my rider commanded gleefully.

"Nay!" I protested.

The boy burst out in giggles. "That's not how horsies say it!"

•

After church, Sander said, "We have the whole day and the whole city at our disposal. Where shall we go?"

"You decide."

"Well, there's a zoo in the Tower, with lions and tigers and a porpentine, even a camel. But all they do is sleep. We could go to Paul's instead."

"Who is Paul?"

"*Saint* Paul's. It's a cathedral. I'll pay for the crossing."

Though a cathedral did not sound like the height of excitement to me, I had no better suggestion. It was another cobweb day, and by the time we crossed the Thames we looked as though we had swum it. Sander's spirits were not dampened in the least. His long legs carried him so swiftly up the hill that I had to fairly trot to keep up. At last we came to the huge cathedral which had attracted my awe the night of my arrival.

"St. Paul's," Sander said. "The center of things."

So now I stood in the center of the center of the universe. I stared about, openmouthed, like the greenest plowboy. The chaotic courtyard of the cathedral was packed with people and vendors' booths. Voices hung in the air as densely as the misty rain. I felt the urge to hold my breath as we plunged into the sea of bodies.

"Keep a firm hold on your wallet," Sander called over the clamor.

I laughed mirthlessly. "I've naught left to steal," I said.

"You want to go up in the tower? I'll pay."

"What's there?"

"A good view of the city. And a few bats." The view from the top of Paul's was, indeed, a good one. Sander pointed out the roofs of the queen's London residence far off to the west, and the Tower prison to the east. Between the two lay more buildings than a man could count. The streets were as crooked and wayward as country streams, dissecting the city not into square blocks but into convoluted shapes of all sizes.

"Beautiful, isn't it?" said Sander.

"It's like a maze. How in heaven's name do you find your way about?"

Sander laughed. "It's easy, when you've grown up in it."

"And you like it?"

"Of course. Don't you?"

"Perhaps I'm just not used to it yet."

"You'll come to like it." He put a hand on my shoulder. I was not used to being touched in a comradely way either, and I flinched. "Sorry," he said. "I forget that the height makes people nervous."

"Aye," I said. "Let's go back down."

The courtyard was no place for a person who was shy of being touched. I lost sight of Sander temporarily but caught up with him again at a bookseller's stall. "Here," he said. "Have a look at this."

Displayed prominently were a number of plays and poems written by "Wm. Shaksper." "Is that our Mr. Shakespeare?"

"Of course."

Eagerly I searched for a copy of *The Tragedy of Hamlet*, then realized that of course if it were bound and printed like these Simon Bass would never have gone to the trouble to send me and Falconer here; he would simply have bought one.

They say that if you mention the devil's name, he is likely to appear. As I turned away from the bookstall, I found that, by thinking his name, I had somehow conjured up Falconer, and to my dismay, he was headed directly for us.

I could not have said whether or not he saw me. As always, his hood sheltered his face. He was pushing his way impatiently through the crowd, but then he always did that. Perhaps it was not too late to avoid him. I plunged into the shifting maze of people. Sander shouted after me, "Widge! Where are you going?"

I did not bother to reply; I only pressed on, burrowing through the tangle of arms and legs like a hare through briars. At last I found daylight at the edge of the courtyard and turned to look back.

Falconer was a tall man, and I could see the tip of his hood bobbing through the crowd. "Gog's blood!" I murmured. He was onto me for certain, and he'd want the script, and perhaps my blood as well. No excuses, he'd said. There was nothing for me to do but run, and no way to run but through the cathedral graveyard.

Though I did not care for the company of dead folk, it was easier to make my way through them. I slipped as quietly as I could between headstones and crypts. The earth was soft from the rain and, in places, from being recently turned up. It gave way slightly under my feet, making me fear that if I did not move quickly, I would sink down into the realm of the dead.

Shuddering, I broke into a trot, never pausing until I reached solid ground. When I peered back through the drizzle, I thought I spied a dark figure weaving among the tombstones. I began to run again, with no goal but to get away. I trotted down one unknown street, then another, sending up sprays of water with each step.

Finally I sank exhausted onto a doorstep. If I hadn't lost Falconer by now, I never would. Unfortunately, I had lost myself as well. I had no idea in which direction Southwark lay. South, of course, but with the sun so well concealed, who could say where that was?

It stood to reason, though, that if I followed the water in the gutters and kept a downhill course, I would eventually run into the Thames as well. How I would get to the far side was another matter. I would have to cross that bridge, or lack of one, when I came to it.

As it turned out, my reasoning was seriously flawed. After only a few minutes' walk, I came to the massive wall that encircled the city. Even I knew that the wall did not run between St. Paul's and the Thames. But by now I was so disoriented that I kept on that street, which was at least broad and well traveled.

Finally I found the good sense to ask an old farmer to point me in the right direction. "Turn left at the next chance," he said, "and follow your nose 'til you wets your toes." I thanked him and hurried on.

The thoroughfare onto which I turned seemed innocuous enough at first, but after a time I noticed that each block was a bit more dismal-looking than the last. Before long the street began to seem less like the path to the river than like a descent into hell.

The prosperous merchants and busy tradesmen had disappeared, and in their place were coarse women and menacing men, bands of noisy, grimy children and scores of beggars.

Lining both sides of the street were ramshackle booths and huts constructed of any material that would keep out the weather—hides, sticks, mud. My impulse was to turn and retrace my steps, but I told myself that I could not possibly be far from the river now, so I kept on, dodging piles of muck.

I did not see the two youths until they were directly before me, blocking my path. My immediate impression was that they were large—large of body, with large grinning mouths and large daggers at their belts. Separately, each would have been daunting; together they were terrifying. I stepped back. They stepped forward. I stepped aside. They followed.

"Wh-what do you want?"

"What have you got?" one of them said.

"Naught but the clothes on me back."

He fingered the hilt of his dagger. "We'll have that, then."

I took a few more backward steps, preparing to run. "You won't get far," the boy said. "There's not a man or woman in sight that won't help catch you. We're all one big family here, you see. And we don't like strangers."

"I was—I was just passing through."

"Well, then you've got to pay a passing-through fee." He drew his dagger. "Now, what will it be? Your clothing? Or your ears?"

"Neither," said a voice behind them. The large boys turned, and I took immediate advantage of the distraction. For the second time that day I was on the run, and this time I was far from fresh. Hands reached out to stay me, but I was a confirmed Master of Dodging, and left them with a handful of air.

I expected at any moment to hear the boys thundering after me. Instead I heard my name being called. "Widge! Wait, Widge!"

I raced on, nearly blind with panic and fatigue. How had they learned my name?

"Widge!" the voice called again, high and clear. "Wait! It's me!"

I slowed and half-turned. The two bully boys were nowhere in sight. Instead a slighter and far more welcome figure was chasing after me. "Julian?" I gasped. I stumbled over some obstacle and fell to my knees, struggling for breath. Julian reached me and held out a hand. I pushed it away. "I can manage."

"Yes, well, you wouldn't have managed if I hadn't happened to show up just then, would you? Come." He guided me to a booth with grain sacks piled against it. "Mind if we rest here a bit, Hugh?" he asked the man within the booth.

"Anyfing you axe, m'dear," the man said.

"You seem to be kenned here," I observed when my breath had caught up with me.

"Known, you mean? I should hope so. It's where I was born and raised. Alsatia, we call it."

"You grew up *here*?" I looked at our squalid surroundings, then at Julian, whose appearance and manner spoke of better things.

He shrugged. "There's worse places."

"None that I've seen."

"Watch what you say, or you may never leave—not standing up at any rate."

I glanced about nervously and got to my feet. "I'll leave now, then, I wis." I pointed down the street. "The river's that way?"

"I may as well go with you. It's only an hour or so until curfew anyway."

"But you said you lived here."

"No longer. Not since I began my prenticeship three years ago. I live with Mr. Phillips and his wife, now."

"And your parents . . . they don't mind?"

Julian gave a humorless laugh, but said nothing.

I looked back over my shoulder. "How is it you escaped those two back there so easily?"

"They wouldn't dare touch a hair of my head. I've got friends here that would cut their ears off, and they know it."

I rubbed at my own ears instinctively. "They came near to cutting mine off. I should thank you."

"Yes," he said. "You should."

"Well," I said. "Thanks, then."

"You're welcome."

I truly was thankful, but at the same time I resented the fact that he'd had to rescue me. Ever since I'd come to London, I'd been getting into situations from which someone else had had to extract me. I was weary of feeling foolish and helpless and useless. I had failed even to make fruitful use of the one skill I did possess—the art of charactery.

When we descended the rain-slick stairs to the water, Julian asked, "Do you have passage money?"

"Nay," I said, feeling helpless yet again.

He handed a wherryman two pennies and four farthings. As we pushed out into the river, he said, "You can repay me when you get your wages."

"You mean—I'm to be paid?"

"When you get through your trial period. It's only three shillings a week, but it's better than nothing. Although, come to that, I suppose I'd do it for nothing."

"You would? Why?"

"Why?" he repeated, with a puzzlement equal to my own. "If you don't know, you won't make much of a prentice, much less a player."

"I won't in any case."

"Not with that attitude. The only ones who succeed are the ones who want it so badly that nothing will keep them from it."

That was hard for me to imagine. I had never bothered to want anything that badly, for I knew it was no use. In the past few days, I'd gotten glimpses of a world very different from the one I was used to, a world I might have wished to be a part of but knew I never could. What was the good in longing for something you could not have? Life was full enough of disappointments, without making more.

Once on the south bank, Julian said, "You can find your way to Mr. Pope's from here?"

"I'm not wholly helpless," I said indignantly.

"I'm glad to hear that."

At Mr. Pope's house, everyone was seated at supper. Mr. Pope lifted his shaggy eyebrows in surprise as I entered. "Well. I supposed we had seen the last of you."

"Why?"

"You wouldn't be the first prentice who's run off. Sander said you'd found your first day not quite to your liking."

"That may be. But I'm not one to quit."

He nodded and smiled slightly. "Good, good. Perhaps you'd best change before you come to the table. You look like a drowned cat."

As I climbed the stairs to our room, Sander came up behind me. "Why did you run off like that? Is something wrong?"

"Nay," I said. "It's naught."

"You can tell me, Widge. I can keep a secret."

For a fleeting moment, I was tempted to open up to him. But how could I? If I did, I would be burning both my bridges. I could never finish my mission for Simon Bass, but neither could I go on being a prentice, once they had learned the truth about me. I shook my head. "It's naught."

He sighed. "I can't be your friend if you won't talk to me."

"I never asked you to be my friend. I never asked for anything." The moment I spoke the words, I regretted them, but I could hardly take them back. Besides, they carried a certain truth. I didn't want him, or any of the players, to be my friend, for I would only have to betray them. And yet some part of me wondered how it would be to have a friend, and to be one.

Blinking, Sander backed away, down the stairs. "Very well," he said in a hurt voice. "I was only trying to help."

I spent as much time as I reasonably could drying off and donning my old clothing, which had been washed without my knowing. When I came downstairs, everyone had left the dining room except Mistress Willingson, who cheerfully set before me a plate of food she had kept warm on the back of the stove.

My day of rest had proved far from restful, nor did I get much rest that night. Each time I fell asleep, I dreamed of a hooded figure pursuing me, and woke in a sweat. As we started for the Globe in the morning, I was heartened to see that, for a change, the sky was clear. But my small delight vanished when we arrived to find that our morning's task was to whitewash the roof thatch.

"Gog's bread!" I grumbled as we climbed the ladder. "Why does the thatch ha' to be made *white*?"

Sander laughed. "It's to keep it from catching fire again."

"Would that it had burned to the ground," I muttered.

Sander pulled up the bucket of whitewash. "What's that?"

"I said, would that we could do this from the ground."

I stuck my long-handled brush in the bucket and made a

few grudging passes at the thatch, then paused and looked out over the plain of red-tiled roofs below me. "Why did they not make this one of tile?"

"Too much of an expense."

"Aye, and it won't cost them a thing if we breaks our necks." As I made another careless swipe at the rough reeds, I spotted on the road below a cloaked figure that I momentarily took to be Falconer. So startled was I that I lost my hold on the brush. It skittered across the thatch and plummeted to the yard three storeys below. "Oh, Holy Mother."

"What's wrong now?"

"I've lost me brush." I stared gloomily after it. Half the yard was eclipsed from my view. Into the half I could see stepped a man with a large white splotch on one shoulder of his dark brown doublet.

"Who is that up there?" the man called.

"It's Widge!" I replied, in a voice as high and unsteady as my perch.

"Who?"

"Widge! The new boy!"

"Well, we don't need the yard whitewashed, Widge, nor the players."

"Aye, sir." I turned to Sander, who was holding a hand over his mouth to stifle his laughter. "It's not funny! It struck someone."

"Who was it? Not Mr. Burbage, I hope?"

"I don't ken. A wight wi' long, dark hair and a pointy beard."

Sander bit his lip and raised his eyebrows. "Mr. Shakespeare."

"Oh, gis. Will 'a ha' me dismissed, do you wis?"

"Not very like. He's a bit prickly at times, but not mean-spirited. Best go fetch your brush."

Before I climbed down, I took another look toward the road. Falconer—if indeed it had been he—was not in sight.

We whitewashed no more than the fourth part of the roof before the church bells rang terce, the hour for our lessons to begin. There were fencing exercises, made slightly more tolerable by the fact that Nick was gone—no one seemed to know where or why. After fencing, one of the hired men, a former apothecary's apprentice named Richard, instructed us in the art of painting our faces. As I sat before the looking glass brushing cochineal on my cheeks, a gypsyish-looking man with a high forehead and a mane of curly black hair came up behind me.

"A likely looking lot of lissome ladies, eh, Mr. Shakespeare?"

"Very fetching." Mr. Shakespeare glanced down at me. "Have a care, now. You don't want that brush to escape you." I flushed with embarrassment. "There, you see, you've reddened your whole face."

"I'm sorry about the whitewash," I murmured.

"It will wash," he said. "A pity it did not fall a bit to the left. You'd have saved me the trouble of whiting my face for today's performance." His words puzzled me until I recalled his role as the ghost. So *Hamlet* was scheduled for this very afternoon, and here was I with no table-book in which to set it down. "That was meant to be a jest," Mr. Shakespeare said.

"Sorry."

He shook his head. "Thank heaven my audience is not made up of such sobersides. Sander, see that this lad is given instructions in laughing."

Sander grinned. "Yes, sir."

When Mr. Shakespeare had gone, Richard looked us over critically. "Very good, Julian. Sander, too much black about the eyes. You look as though you're consumptive. Widge, a little less whitewash next time, and smooth it out under your chin. Clean up now; it's nearly dinner time." As we wiped our faces, he said, "It's sunny today, so wear a hat outside, else we'll be having to put a pound of white on, to hide the freckles. Remember, it's easier to tan a hide than to hide a tan."

Sander elbowed me in the ribs. "Laugh," he said.

As it happened, Sander would have done well to leave his face made up. When the time came for the performance, Nick failed to appear. Mr. Heminges came back and took the book from Sander's hands. "G-go and g-et yourself up in Nick's costume. D-do you know his lines?"

"I've a nodding acquaintance with them," Sander said, his voice sounding uncharacteristically nervous.

"Have the p-property master give you his side, and read from it if you m-must."

"Yes, sir." Sander hurried off.

Mr. Heminges looked after him, rubbing his forehead as though it pained him. Then he glanced over at me and, to my astonishment, thrust the book into my hands. "Widge, you'll hold the b-book. If anyone seems l-lost for a line, f-feed them a few words. Not a whole m-mouthful, mind you, just a t-taste, to start their chawbones m-moving. Can you do that?"

I closed my gaping mouth and said "Aye," and he strode off to deal with some other crisis. For a moment all I could do was stare at the book in disbelief. All the fretting and scheming I'd done over how I would copy the play, and suddenly here it was, handed over to me in one piece, without the slightest effort on my part. All I had to do was tuck it under my arm and turn and walk out of the theatre.

Everyone else in the company was occupied with some task. No one would notice. And yet, what if they *did* notice? My intentions would be obvious, and all chance of completing my mission would be lost. I turned toward the door, hesitated, turned back, started for the door again—and encountered Sander sweeping from the tiring-room, dressed as Hamlet's mother.

"How do I look?" he asked anxiously, pushing at his voluminous wig.

Far from calm myself, I gave him a cursory look up and down. "Well enough, I wis. Wait. Your sleeve's coming off."

"Pin it on, would you?"

"Yes, very well," I said irritably. The task required both

hands, and I glanced about, wondering what to do with the play book. "Here." I handed it to Sander.

"Make haste," he begged. "I'm due on the stage."

"I'm trying!" I snapped, fumbling with the pins. "Why don't they just sew these on?"

"You can change the dress about this way, put different sleeves on. Have you got it?"

"Almost."

There was a flourish of trumpets above the stage. "It'll have to do. There's my cue." He started for the stage entrance.

"The book!" I whispered urgently.

He shoved it into my hands and dashed for the doorway, tripped himself up in his hem, recovered, hoisted the skirts in a very unladylike fashion, and burst through the curtain onto the stage.

"Ah, Gertrude," the king said. "So glad you could join us." The audience guffawed at this spontaneous addition to the script. The king then launched into a speech that promised to be lengthy. Time to go, I thought.

Suddenly the king broke off, his arm upraised, as though frozen in place. I froze, too, aware that something was amiss, but not quite sure what. A few snickers arose from the audience. The king cast a perturbed glance in my direction, and I realized he had forgotten his line.

I yanked the book open. Before I could locate the proper passage, Laertes closed the breach: "Sorry to interrupt, my lord, but I beg your leave and favor to return to France."

I looked about anxiously, certain that someone would swoop down to snatch the book from my incompetent hands. But everyone was too busy to notice. If I had had the sense that God gave sheep, I would have made my escape at that moment. But the king had another attack of forgetfulness. This time I had the book open to the place. "Take thy fair hour!" I called out, too loudly, drawing another snicker from the audience. The king snatched up the cue and ran with it. Behind his back, Sander made a gesture of approval at me. I couldn't help smiling.

Ah, well, I thought; I can just as easily stay and help out here, and still slip away before the finish of the play.

When the scene was over, Sander came to where I stood. "How did I do?"

"Whist!" I said. "You'll make me lose me place!"

"It wouldn't be the first time," he teased. "Come now, truly. How was I?"

"You were magnificent," I said dryly. "You fairly lit up the stage."

He delivered a most unqueenly swat to my arm. "You dolt!"

"Ouch! Will you go faddle wi' your pins or something, and let me do me job?"

"All right, then. It's plain I'll get no useful criticism from you."

"You don't want criticism. You want praise."

"Suppose I do. It would scarcely kill you." His voice had lost some of its jesting tone.

"What do you care what I think?"

"I thought we were friends."

"Oh." I thought of how my words had stung him the day before. "Aye." I dropped my gaze to the script, as though it might provide my next line, but it was of no help.

Just then, the rear door of the playhouse flew open, and Nick burst in, disheveled and panting. "Am I late?" he gasped.

"By about half an act," Sander said.

Nick glared at him. "What are you doing in my costume?"

"Playing your part, actually."

"Well, take it off!" When Sander made no move to comply, Nick tugged at the bodice. "Did you hear me, Cooke? Get out of my costume!"

"Soft!" I said. "You'll be heard out there!"

"Go eat hay, Horse." He turned back to Sander. "Do I have to shake you out of it?"

"You're in no shape to go on," Sander said, calmly. "You've got a bit of a beard, for one thing. And, from the smell of your breath, I'd say a bit of beer as well."

"I'll beard you," Nick growled. He yanked at the bodice, pulling loose the hooks at the side. Sander stumbled backward and tripped on the hem. His head struck the edge of the stage doorway with an audible thump.

I had been doing foolish things with great frequency the past few days—and most of my life, for that matter—and I now did another. I swung the heavy bound book into the small of Nick's back. He let out a grunt of pain and turned on me, like a baited bear turning on the hounds. He lashed out at me, and the blow would have caught me full in the face had I not been so adept at ducking. Instead, it glanced off the top of my pate.

Before he could swing again, he was seized from behind by Jack, the cannoneer. "What's going on here?" Jack demanded in a loud whisper.

Nick shook loose from him. "He's trying to steal my part."

Jack scowled at me. "You, eh? I knew you was up to no good."

Sander got to his feet, rubbing the back of his head. "It's me he's accusing, Jack. Nick, if you're not here, somebody has to go on for you, you know that."

Mr. Armin hurried up. "What are you boys doing? Your clamor carried all the way to the tiring-room. Nick, where have you been?"

"I overslept," Nick said sullenly.

"Until nones?" He looked the boy over distastefully. "Go home. You're obviously not fit to perform. We'll discuss your fine later."

"I've nothing to pay a fine with. I lost it all at dice."

"We'll take it out of your future wages, then—if there are any. Go on, now." Mr. Armin waved a hand at us. "Back to work, boys. You're doing well, Sander. You too, Widge."

Though it was small enough praise, it took me off

guard. I was as unaccustomed to praise as I was to having a friend, or being one. The pleasant feeling it gave me was unaccustomed, too, and gave me a small hint of what the players must experience when the audience applauded their efforts.

For the first time, Jack noticed that I was holding the play book. He snatched it from my hands. "What are *you* doing with that?"

"Mr. Heminges gave it to me."

"Well, I'm taking it back. I don't trust you."

"But you can't—!" I started to protest. Sander pulled me away.

"Let it be. No point in making another commotion."

"But that was me job!"

"Don't worry, you'll have it back soon enough." With a grin, he whispered, "Jack can scarcely read his own name."

I made no reply. There was no way I could tell him how important that book was to me, or why. As I headed for the tiring-room, I cursed myself for having hesitated and lost my best chance to hand the book of the play over to Falconer. I would have to keep him waiting yet a while, and he was not the sort who would relish it. Nor, I thought, was he the sort, when I finally did deliver, to praise me for a job well done.

16

In the tiring-room, Mr. Heminges was putting more white in his beard for his part as Polonius, and Mr. Shakespeare, dressed all in armor, was touching up his ghostly white makeup. Mr. Heminges gave me a startled look. "Wh-where is the b-book?"

"Jack insisted on taking it over," Sander answered for me.

"Lord h-help us."

"Still," said Mr. Shakespeare, "it's better than I feared. In view of his habit of dropping things, I expected that Widge had let it fall into Hell."

"Hell?" I echoed.

"Our word for the cellar beneath the stage." Sander

leaned close to me. "Don't listen to him. He's just heckling you."

"I ken that."

Mr. Heminges sighed. "I'm due on the stage. We'll settle this later." He dusted the excess powder from his beard and started for the door, pausing long enough to say to Mr. Shakespeare, "You wouldn't care to t-trade duties for a t-time, would you, Will? I'll write the p-plays, and you run the c-company?"

Mr. Shakespeare considered a moment. "I suppose that's no more absurd than letting Jack hold the book." He turned his gaze back to the looking glass. The man who played Laertes came into the room and struck up a conversation with Sander. I let my thoughts wander, and my eyes with them.

Because of his helmet, I could not see Mr. Shakespeare's face directly, only his reflection in the glass. He had finished repairing his ghostly pallor and now sat staring at his reflection, not as if assessing his appearance, but as though the looking glass were a scrying glass and, like the gypsies he resembled, he was seeing into another time or place. And perhaps he was. Perhaps he was preparing his next play in his mind, even as he prepared himself physically for this one.

Before I could look away, his gaze caught mine in the glass. He frowned. "Do you have nothing better to do than lounge about in the tiring-room?"

"Well, I was to hold the book, sir."

"Then you should have held it more firmly." He rose and strode from the room, his armor clanking.

"What was that about?" said Sander.

"I hardly ken. Was 'a truly cross wi' me, do you wis?"

"You can't tell sometimes, with him."

"That's so," said the man who played Laertes. "He's a hard one to know. They say that, in his younger days, he was a good companion—and he still can be on occasion. But much of the time he's withdrawn and pensive. If having a touch of genius also means having so strong a dose of melancholy, I'll settle for merely being extremely talented."

"And extremely conceited," Sander said. "By the by, you two haven't met, have you? Widge, this is Chris Beeston. Not so long ago he was a lowly prentice like us."

Beeston held out a hand, which I took hesitantly. "Widge, eh? You're the one who made me do a little jig to cover for Henry when he dropped his lines? How is it you're not out there now, holding the book?"

"It's not me fault!" I said. "Why does everyone fret so about the book?"

"Because," Beeston said, "they have a way of ending up in the wrong hands if we're not careful."

"What do you mean?" I said, though I knew well enough.

"He means sometimes they get stolen," Sander said.

"Oh?" I did not care for the direction this conversation was taking. "Who would want to steal a play?"

"Other theatre companies." Beeston leaned forward and lowered his voice. "I've heard it said that's why Will Kempe left the company. They say he made off with the book of *As You Like It*, and sold it to a touring company in Leicester."

"Leicester?" I said, my voice sounding strained.

Beeston nodded. "The man who runs the Leicester company was with the Chamberlain's Men for a time, back when I was still doing girls' parts—a fellow named Simon Bass." I had feared this was coming, and had my face ready so that it did not betray me—or so I hoped. "He gave me my first fencing lessons." Beeston held out his right hand. "I've still got a scar there, where he struck me. I never knew him well, but there was always something about him that didn't go down right. I never quite trusted him. One thing I will admit, he knew more about makeup than anyone else in the company. His Shylock in *Merchant of Venice* is one of the most astounding transformations I've ever seen. But then, perhaps it wasn't all acting." His voice became even softer. "They say his name is really Simon Bashevi, and he's a Jew himself."

"A jewel?" I echoed. The others burst out laughing. "What?"

"A *Jew*," Beeston said. "Don't you know what a Jew is?"

"Of course. I heard you wrong, that's all." In truth, the concept was hazy in my mind. I knew that Falconer had killed a man for calling him one. To mask my ignorance, I repeated what Falconer had said. "There are no Jews in England. Only former Jews."

"Well, that's so," Beeston said. "After what Lopez did."

Though I had no notion who Lopez was, I nodded knowingly. It was not until a month or two later that I learned how Dr. Lopez had tried to poison the queen and been executed, and how all other Jews had been forced to renounce their religion or be banished.

Sander jumped up from the bench then, as suddenly as if stuck by one of his dress pins. "The cock crow!"

"The what?"

"The cock crow! Come!" I followed him from the tiring-room. "I missed the first one while I was dressing, and Jack is sure to forget this one." Jack stood by the stage entrance, peering at the book as though he'd lost his place long ago.

He gave us a sullen glance. "I don't need no help."

"I wasn't offering any," Sander told him. "I've come to do the cock crow."

"I can do it well enough," Jack said. "Where is it?" He ran a finger down the page. "Cock crows. There. Off with you, now."

"I've practiced it," Sander insisted. "I'll do it."

"I know how to crow!" Jack said.

On the stage, Mr. Shakespeare gave the cue in his hollow ghost's voice: "Adieu, adieu, adieu. Remember me." Both Jack and Sander opened their mouths. One let out a sound reminiscent of a squalling baby; the other sounded uncannily like a stuck pig. Either by itself would have been startling; together they were positively unnerving.

I shook a finger in the ear that had borne the brunt of the noise. "Do you truly wis that's how a cock sounds?"

"I suppose you can do it better," Sander said.

"I'm a country wight, remember? I ken what a cock sounds like, and that's not it."

Jack scowled at me. "As it so happens," he said, "this was a *Danish* cock."

Sander and I looked at one another, then broke into fits of laughter. We had to stagger back to the tiring-room holding our hands over our mouths and close the door, lest we infect the audience. It had been a long while since I'd laughed so freely, if indeed I ever had.

By all accounts, Jack did not furnish a single word to assist the poor players, who were forced to invent or to omit whole passages. He was not permitted to hold the book again. Neither, unfortunately, was I—not because I was not trusted, but because our book keeper recovered and resumed his duties. So I had no further chance to carry off the script.

I could not honestly say that I regretted it. The longer I stayed with the company, and the longer I was away from Falconer, the less incentive I felt to complete my mission. I had not forgotten the reward promised me, but that, too, prompted me less and less. All I had was Bass's word in the matter, and judging from what Chris Beeston had said, his word was not worth much. One thing I did know from hard experience: a master's promise to a prentice is likely to be redeemed only at the last Lammas, as they say—which is to say never.

When a week went by, and Falconer had made no attempt to contact me, I convinced myself that he had lost patience and returned to Leicester, to report to Simon Bass. Still, I stuck close to the theatre and, in my free hours, to Mr. Pope's. Though Falconer was impatient, I had the feeling he was used to getting what he wanted, one way or another.

I applied myself to my daily tasks and lessons at the theatre and, to my surprise, began to actually enjoy them. Dr. Bright had trained me as a man might train a dumb beast, through repetition, reinforced by beatings. Here the method was different. We were given credit for some intelligence. We were expected to learn each technique quickly and to practice what we had learned on our own until it became second nature.

At the end of that week, I was, to my astonishment, given a small part to play, that of the Messenger in *The Spanish Tragedy*. "I have a letter to your lordship," I was to say, and "From Pedringano that's imprisoned," and then "Aye, my good lord." That was the extent of my role. I swear by Saint Pintle that I practiced those lines a thousand times at the very least. I believe I may have repeated them in my sleep.

Sander bore with me and the infinite variations I employed in saying my lines, and my inability to say the name Pedringano properly, until he could bear it no longer. One morning as I stood before the looking glass in our room saying, "Perigando. Predinago. Pedigango," he reached the limits of his tolerance.

"Widge! For all the loves on Earth! What will you do when they give you an entire speech?"

I stared at him in dismay. "Oh, gis! Do you think they will?"

Sander began to laugh. "What did you just say?"

"I said, will they give me a whole speech?"

"No, you didn't. You said, 'Do you *think* they will?' Not do you *wis*, but do you *think*." He slapped me on the back, and for a change, I did not flinch. "My boy, I believe you're turning into a Londoner."

"Gog's bread," I muttered, not knowing whether to be pleased or alarmed. "I hope not."

The play was to be put before an audience on Wednesday. Tuesday night I scarcely slept. Toward daybreak, as I sat up, reading in the half-light one of the ballad-sheets on the walls, Sander woke and peered drowsily at me. "What are you doing?"

"Fretting, mostly."

He clucked his tongue. "It's only three lines, Widge."

"All the more cause to fret. An I say them wrong, I'll ha' no chance to redeem meself."

Sander sighed. "Do you want me to play the lines for you?"

"You've a part of your own."

"I can play more than one. It's done all the time."

"Nay. Nay, I'm not one to quit. I'll do it—somehow."

He yawned and lay back down. After a moment, I said, "It gets easier, doesn't it? Playing a part?"

Sander did not reply. He had fallen asleep.

Eventually I succumbed to sleep myself and woke with the sun on my face. I shook my head to dispel the dream that had filled it. In the dream, I made my maiden entrance upon the stage, and the audience at once broke into gales of applause and laughter. Pleased at having created such a sensation without opening my mouth, I smiled and bowed deeply—to discover that I stood before them *in puris naturalibus*, that is to say naked as a worm.

"Oh, Sander, what a dream!" I said. But Sander was not in bed, nor in the room. Then it came to me that if the sun was up, I should be too, long since. I scrambled into my clothing and hurried downstairs. Goodwife Willingson was feeding the smaller children. "Good morning, Widge!" the boys chorused.

I gulped a bowl of porridge, burning my mouth in my haste, and excused myself. "God buy, Widge!" the boys called after me. I paused long enough to wave to them.

Their enthusiasm made me smile as I closed the door and set out for the theatre.

A hundred yards or so from the house I became aware of another set of footsteps behind me, even swifter than my brisk pace—some fellow player late for morning rehearsal, I guessed.

As I turned to see, a hand seized the neck of my tunic. I was dragged to the side of the road, hoisted like a sack of grain over a low hedge, and flung on my back in the grass.

17

I sat up, dazed and frightened, to find the dark, hooded figure of Falconer crouching over me like some rough beast over its prey. "Where is it?" he demanded, in that harsh and hollow voice.

I tried to rise. "I—I—I've been having trouble—"

He shoved me back. "Trouble? You haven't begun to learn what trouble is! Where is the script?"

"It was—it was stolen from me wallet. By a thief."

"The devil take your lying tongue!" He snatched his dagger from his belt and thrust it under my chin. "The truth, now!"

"It's true!" I cried frantically. "As true as steel, I swear it!"

"Then you've made a new copy for me?"

124

"I'm trying."

"Trying? You think I haven't watched your comings and goings? You've been at the Globe every day, and you've nothing to show for it!"

"I can't do 't wi'out being seen!"

He let out a hiss of disgust and let the tip of the dagger drop an inch or two. Gasping, I rubbed at the spot where it had pricked my skin. "Well," he said, "there's nothing left to do, then, but to take the book."

"I meant to, but they keep such a close watch on it."

"Take it from the trunk. It'll be kept in the property room."

"Suppose it's locked?"

"Break the lock! I want that script, and I am accustomed to getting what I want. Have it for me tonight. I'll be waiting. Understood?"

I nodded, very carefully in view of the dagger so near my chin. Falconer suddenly lifted the point again and pressed it against my chin. "And mark me, boy. Breathe no word of this to anyone, or I'll cut out your wagging tongue." With that he stood, stepped over the hedge, and was gone.

I lay in the grass for some time, my heart clamoring in my chest and my limbs weak as water, before I could compose myself enough to continue on to the playhouse.

When I came through the rear door, Mr. Pope was just making an exit from the stage, his face set in the jolly grin required by his role. When he saw me, he resumed his usual gruff expression. "Ah, Widge, you've decided to join us." He shook his head in mock exasperation. "Give a boy a few lines to say, and he thinks he owns the theatre." As he came nearer, his face took on a look of concern. "Are you well, boy? You look as if you'd eaten a batch of bad oysters. Sander said you'd been upset, but—"

"It's naught," I said. "I ran too hard getting here, that's all."

"There was no need. We can manage without you for an hour or two."

"I ken that. I don't like it thought that I'm shirking me duties."

"No one thought that." He lifted my chin. "What have you done to yourself? You're bleeding."

"Oh, that. I—ah—I stumbled and fell into a hedge."

Mr. Pope pulled his kerchief from his sleeve. "Hold that on it. Now, will you need the morning free to study your daunting part, do you think?"

I flushed. "Nay, I can speak it well enough."

In the practice room, Mr. Armin was strapping a metal plate to Sander's waist. "Just in time, Widge." Mr. Armin tossed a short sword to me. So shaken was I that I dropped it, drawing a derisive laugh from Nick. "We'll have to practice that," Mr. Armin said. "But for the moment, you will all be learning how to die properly."

I had come as close to dying as I cared to for one day, but I kept silent and tried to attend to Mr. Armin's words. "We'll be enlisting you prentices for battle scenes soon.

Your weapons will be blunted, but there will be no protective tips. So, lest you die *too* convincingly, you'll wear a metal plate." He tapped the one at Sander's waist. "It is the responsibility of your adversary to see that he strikes this, and not your gut. Of course, in Nick's case, it may be difficult to avoid." He gave a wry glance at the pronounced belly Nick had begun to develop as a result of his regular carousing.

"Now, you've all seen the small bladders full of sheep's blood which we use. They are tied flat to the plate, and the point of the sword bursts them. We'll try that another time. For now, pair off and take turns being killer and victim." He handed Julian a metal plate. "You and Widge trade blows. Carefully."

"Are you sure he's ready for this, Mr. Armin?" Julian asked anxiously as he strapped on the plate.

"He'll do well enough. Now. Low ward. *Dritta. Riversa. Incartata.*" I thrust under Julian's singlestick; the sword hit the protective plate, but to my astonishment, the plate did not stop it. My momentum carried the hilt forward six inches.

"Oh, God!" I cried. "I've stuck him!"

But Julian did not appear to be stuck. Indeed, he was laughing. "It's your sword. It collapses into the hilt!"

I gaped at him, then at the sword. "It's a trick sword? Why didn't you tell me?"

"And miss the look on your face?"

"I was afeared I'd slain you," I said sulkily.

Julian laid an arm upon my shoulder. I shrugged it off. "Come now, no hard feelings, eh? It was a jest."

We took up our positions again. When I struck Julian this time, he gave a halfhearted groan and clutched at his belly. "You look as though you'd eaten too many sweets, not suffered a mortal wound," Mr. Armin said. "Trade roles, now."

I handed my sword to Julian and strapped on the protective plate. In the school of hard knocks where I had become a Master of Dodging, I had also learned to feign injury, as a way of lessening the severity of a beating. The experience stood me in good stead now. When Julian struck me, I gave a howl of agony and crumpled to the floor, my face a very picture of pain and terror.

"Mother Mary!" Julian breathed. "Are you wounded?" I grinned up at him. He gave me an exasperated nudge with one foot. "You sot!"

"Very dramatic," Mr. Armin said dryly. "No one will even notice the principals, they'll be so busy looking at you."

During our rest time, Julian and I sat against the wall, sipping cups of water. "Well," he said casually, "perhaps you're not such a bad sort after all, for a country wight."

I stared at him. "Is that the London way of giving a compliment?"

He smiled. "I suppose it is."

"In that case, I suppose you're not such a bad sort, either. For a city wight."

"Touch. Your point. So, how do you come to be in London?"

"That's something of a long tale."

"Just give me a brief summary."

"I ran away from me master, that's the long and short of it."

"And your parents?"

"Me mother's long since dead. Me father . . ." I hesitated and then, seeing Julian's sympathetic look, went on. "I don't ken who me father was."

Julian nodded. "We're birds of a feather, then. I lost my mum when I was small, to the plague. And my da is—" He shrugged. "Well, my da will die of the dropsy one day, I've no doubt."

"The dropsy?"

"One of the words we use to mean hanging from Tyburn Tree."

"Hanging? Why? What has 'a done?"

"What *hasn't* he done, you might as well ask. As far as I know, he's never murdered anyone, and I don't suppose he's ever betrayed one of his fellows. Anything else he'll do, if there's money in it. That's why he lets me prentice here— they pay him a small sum yearly."

"Aye? Do you think that—"

"What?"

"Oh, I was just wondering whether me master might be willing to do the same—let me stay on an they paid him a bit."

"You think he'll come after you, then?"

"Aye, I'm afeard 'a will."

"I hope he doesn't," Julian said. "You're just beginning to show some promise."

I felt myself flush. "Do you truly think so?"

Julian grinned. "Well, if you can feign love or compassion half so well as you can feign an agonizing death, you'll be as famous as Burbage."

"I've had no experience in such things," I said. "But I'm willing to learn."

We were kept so busy through the morning that I scarcely had time to dread the afternoon, when I would step onstage and say my three lines. Yet the threat of it hung over my head, along with the more dire threat of Falconer out there, waiting for me to deliver the script.

An hour before the performance I was in costume, not wishing to see my dream come true. I paced about behind the stage muttering "Pedringano, Pedringano" like an incantation.

"Widge," Sander said, "sit somewhere and practice breathing deeply. I'll call you when you're due on the stage."

"An you forget, what then?"

"I won't forget."

Nonetheless, I was unable to sit still. I went on stomping about, repeating my lines and getting in everyone's way until at last Julian took me by the arm. "Come. You're going to help me with my lines for *Satiromastix*."

It did calm me a bit, having something to do, and Sander was as good as his word, though he got me to the stage with a scant half-minute to spare. "Gives you less time to fret," he said. When my cue came, I froze, and he was forced to propel me onto the stage.

My actual moment of glory is a blank in my memory. I must have gotten out my lines, Pedringano and all, without disgracing myself or the company, for afterward, in the tiring-room, I was congratulated by the other players as though I had passed through fire—which, in a sense, I had.

"I remember well my first faltering steps upon the boards," Mr. Pope said.

"I'd no idea they had boards so long ago," Mr. Armin said.

"Oh, we knew how to make boards well enough. It wasn't until your time that we learned how to make an *audience* bored." There was much laughter. "To return to my story, I was given the part of gluttony in a play called *Nature*. I was not so well upholstered in those days, so they strapped a sack of buckram about my waist. Halfway through the play it came loose and descended about my knees, so that I resembled not a glutton so much as a pear with legs."

"I had much the same experience," Mr. Phillips said, "save that I was playing a woman, and it was my bosom which migrated south."

I was enjoying the players' tales so much that I neglected to undress and remove my makeup. When everyone else was ready to leave, I was still wiping off my face paint.

"Want us to wait for you?" Sander asked.

I hesitated. If I was in their company, Falconer could not accost me again. Yet I could not avoid him forever. He had said I must have the script for him that very night, or—well, he had not made it clear what the alternative was, but I knew it would not be pleasant. "Nay," I said, trying to sound casual. "Go on wi'out me. I'll be along."

When they were gone, I sat staring into the looking glass as I had seen Mr. Shakespeare do, pondering my dilemma. All my life I had done what I was told to do without question, without thinking about the right or the wrong of it. This time I couldn't help questioning.

I had no doubt that what Falconer and my master, Simon Bass, were asking me to do was wrong. Even a thief, Julian had said, would not betray his fellows. And if I took the script, I would indeed have betrayed my fellows. I had no desire to do so. They had taken me in and shown me kindness and trust and friendship. I had been alone and friendless a long time and had accepted it as my lot. But in the past weeks, I had learned something of what it meant to have friends, and to be a real prentice, not a mere slave. It was a piece of knowledge late to come and hard-won, and one I did not wish to forget.

Yet I had learned what it means to have an enemy, too. As I scrubbed the makeup from my chin, I wiped the spot where Falconer's dagger had pricked the skin. I flinched.

Another piece of hard-won knowledge I did not care to forget, lest it be impressed upon me again, more forcefully and more permanently.

I turned away from the looking glass. I had been contemplating the matter as if I had a choice. The truth was, if I hoped to save my own skin, I had no choice.

18

By the time I shed my costume and hung it in the wardrobe and dressed in my customary clothing, the light coming through the high windows had faded. I stepped from the tiring-room and looked about and listened. The area behind the stage was deserted.

Cautiously I moved across to the door of the property room. It was unlocked. I stepped inside and pushed it closed behind me, leaving a gap of a hand's breadth to let a bit of light into the windowless room.

It contained half a dozen trunks, several of them secured with locks. There was no way of knowing which one contained the play books. I had long since learned to look for the easiest way of pursuing a task. It would be far easier to look in the unlocked chests first, on the slight chance that one of them might hold the treasure.

I raised the lid of the nearest one. The hinges protested feebly and I halted, fearing someone might still be in the theatre. Hearing nothing, I yanked the lid open and peered inside. Small weapons of all sorts, from bucklers to broadswords, were piled within. I went on to the next trunk.

The light was so far gone that I had to lay the lid back and bend close in order to see. I gasped and stumbled backward in horror. The trunk was packed with parts of human bodies—bloody arms, hands cut off at the wrist, severed heads with staring, sightless eyes.

I knocked against another chest and sat heavily down upon it. Holding a hand over my mouth to muffle my frantic breathing, I gaped at the trunk as though the awful contents might crawl from it. Slowly it came to me that these were mere stage properties, made of plaster and paint, and then I had to keep my hand over my mouth to stifle the relieved laughter that rose in me.

I was suddenly sobered by the sound of footfalls close by. I rolled off the trunk and crouched behind it. The footsteps approached and halted before the door of the property room. For a moment there was utter silence. I held my breath. Then I heard the door swing on its hinges—not open, but closed. The thin shaft of light was eclipsed. The latch clicked; a key rattled in the lock; the bolt slid into place. Then the footsteps retreated. Finally there was a distant, muffled thump—the rear door of the theatre being closed and locked.

I crawled out from behind the trunk and felt my way across the black room, banging painfully against racks of weapons and corners of trunks. As I expected, the door was locked as surely and securely as those locked trunks. If I groped about in the dark long enough, I might manage eventually to break into the book keeper's trunk and liberate the script. But what good would it do me if I was still a prisoner?

In the end, I made no attempt to force the trunks or locate the play book. If discovered here in the morning, I could contrive some explanation of how I came to be shut up in the property room. But even with my skill at lying I would have a hard time explaining broken locks and a missing script.

There was one advantage, at least, in being locked up so securely: Falconer could not get to me. There were also several distinct disadvantages: I had no food, no water, no place to relieve myself, and no bed to sleep in. Such discomforts were not new to me, but lately I had become accustomed to regular meals and soft bedding.

I found by touch a helmet to relieve myself in, and a pile of carpets in one corner of the room to lie down upon and sleep the untroubled sleep of the prisoner who is resigned to his prison.

I woke in the morning to the sound of footsteps, and the property room door being unlocked. Like a mouse, I scrambled for a hiding place, but I need not have bothered. The door was not opened. When I heard the footsteps climb the stairs, I stole across the room and out the door, and thence out of the theatre.

The sun had not yet shown itself, and I hoped I might be at Mr. Pope's in time for breakfast. Fearing that Falconer might lie in wait, I took a roundabout route and came upon Mr. Pope and Sander as they were leaving the house.

"And where have you been the whole night long, my lad?" Mr. Pope demanded.

"Well," I replied, to buy a bit of time, "it's rather a long tale."

"Then you'd best begin at once."

"Well, sir, the truth is, it's . . . it's me old master. 'A hunted me down here—'a kenned how I had me heart set on being a player, you see—and 'a tried to force me to return to Yorkshire wi' him. I went along as far as St. Albans"—such details add credibility to a lie—"where I slipped away, and I've spent the night walking back."

"Saints' mercy," said Sander. "You must be exhausted."

Mr. Pope was more skeptical. "You walked all the way from St. Albans? That's upwards of twenty miles."

"Nay, nay," I said quickly. "I never walked the whole time. A farmer brought me half that way on his cart. I even slept a bit on his load of straw." I brushed imaginary chaff from my tunic.

This seemed to satisfy him, and he grew more solicitous. "Have you eaten, then?"

"Aye," I said, not wishing to try his patience. "The good farmer shared his bread and cheese wi' me." Would that I could have lied so convincingly to my complaining stomach.

As we walked on, Sander hung back and whispered, "I didn't tell him you were gone. He just noticed. He was anxious about you."

"About me? Truly?"

Sander nodded. "He takes the welfare of his boys very seriously."

I was accustomed to being called someone's "boy." Like the term "his man," it can mean you are the servant, or chattel, of that person. But the way Sander used the word, it implied something more, something better—that I was not merely part of a household, but part of a family.

My empty belly made the morning's lessons seem interminable. We were well into them before Nick appeared, looking as though he'd slept in his clothing, and at the same time as though he hadn't slept at all. Mr. Armin left us to perform our *passatas*, and drew Nick into a corner, where they had a lengthy conversation. As their tempers mounted, so did their voices.

"I'm not a child!" Nick was saying. "When will you stop treating me as one?"

"When you stop behaving as one! Drinking and gaming until all hours is not the mark of a man!"

"Neither is wearing skirts and prancing about the stage like a woman!"

"Ah, that's it, is it? You feel you're ready for men's roles, do you?"

"Well, I—" Nick hesitated. "I'm sick of playing a girl, that's all." He rubbed at the stubble on his cheeks. "And I'm sick of being thought a callow boy wherever I go, because I'm forced to shave my beard."

"So you feel you're ready to move from prentice to hired man. Are you quite certain you've learned everything you need to know?"

Nick's voice faltered. "Perhaps . . . perhaps not everything."

"No, I think not. Come. Let's try to fill in what you lack, so that when the time comes for you to play a man's part, you'll be ready." Mr. Armin glanced at the three of us, who had been eavesdropping. "You lot have far more to learn than he does," he called. "Get back to work. Fifty more *passatas*."

As we thrust over and over at the unyielding wall, I whispered to Sander, "An Nick is so much of a trouble, why do you not give him the chuck?"

Sander gave me a puzzled look. "The chuck?"

"Aye. Throw him out."

Sander stopped to wipe his brow. "Would you throw out your brother, if you had one?"

"I don't have one."

"But if you did?"

"That's different."

"Not really. Don't you see? The theatre is a sort of family and, like him or no, Nick is a part of it." A few weeks before, I would not have understood his meaning, but now I felt I did. "Besides," Sander went on, "he's having a bad time just now, that's all. He'll come around."

"Perhaps," I said doubtfully. "I'd just prefer 'a didn't come around me."

Later, as we were on our way downstairs, Will Sly stopped me. "Mr. Heminges wants to see you."

"Me?"

"Do you know another Widge? He's in the property room."

"The—the property room?"

"Has anyone checked this boy's ears? I believe he's a trifle deaf."

"Perhaps you're not saying things properly," Julian countered. "You haven't been drinking, have you?"

Will grinned. "No more than usual."

"Ah, that's the problem, then. You've not lubricated your chawbones."

I was not in a mood to appreciate their jests. What business could Mr. Heminges have with me, particularly in the property room? I could think of but one possible topic, and it was not one I was eager to discuss.

19

I considered walking on past the property room and out the rear door. What kept me from it was the thought of Falconer. If I had to answer to someone, I preferred that it be the person least likely to cut my throat.

I halted before the property room door, like a condemned man at the foot of the gallows. Mr. Heminges sat within at a table, writing figures in a ledger. He looked up and beckoned to me. "C-come in, Widge. I'm just d-doing accounts. My least favorite d-duty, but a n-necessary one." He sprinkled sand on the fresh ink, blew it off, and closed the ledger. "N-now. I understand you were in a b-bit of t-trouble last night."

My stomach knotted up. "Aye. But it wasn't me own fault—"

"I know that. T-Thomas gave me a full account."

"Thomas?"

"Mr. Pope."

"Oh." How could Mr. Pope have known about my attempted theft? Had he been the one who locked me in the room?

"This is a serious p-problem, but not an unusual one."

"It's not?"

"N-no. In f-fact several of our prentices have done the same."

"Truly? What did you do to them?"

"D-do to them?" Now it was Mr. Heminges's turn to sound bewildered.

"Were they not punished?"

Mr. Heminges laughed. "For running off from their m-masters? If we t-took on only those b-boys whose masters have agreed to hand them over, we'd b-be rather short on p-prentices. M-most would as soon hand them over to the d-Devil."

It came to me then, almost too late, that we were talking of two entirely different matters. I was concerned with what I'd actually done, and he with the lie I'd concocted to cover it. I hastened to scramble out of the hole I'd dug for myself. I shook my head glumly. "Me master seemed bent on having me back."

"This is England, not China. A man has the right to choose his own p-path. If you truly wish to stay on here, and p-prove yourself able, we will stand with you. If your m-master comes for you, we will offer him the usual f-fee to b-buy off your obligation, and he may take or l-leave it. But we'll see that he leaves *you*, in any c-case. Does that suit you?"

I nodded, so taken aback by this offer of kindness where I had looked for wrath that I could scarcely speak. "Aye. It does indeed."

"Good. G-go back to your lessons, then." I turned to go. "Oh, by the by. They tell me you m-managed to deliver your three lines without f-fainting yesterday. We'll have to try you with four or f-five next time, eh?"

"I don't ken, sir. I'm not sure I could bear it."

He laughed, taking this for a jest, and I let him. "One more th-thing, Widge. I've f-fancied all morning that I smelled something r-rotten, as Mr. Shakespeare says, but my n-nose isn't what it was. Do you smell anything?"

I did indeed, but it took me a moment to recall what it was—the helmet I had used as a chamber pot. I felt my face go red. "A dead rat, most like," I said, and quickly turned away.

For the second time that day, I had been made to feel that I was among people who cared about me and my welfare. My guilt at the thought of betraying him and the rest of the company came back, stronger than ever.

They would stand with me, Mr. Heminges had said. But he said it without knowing the true source of my troubles.

If anyone came after me, it would not be Dr. Bright nor my current master, Simon Bass, who might be willing to listen to reason. It would be the formidable and unreasonable Falconer.

I did not wish to endanger anyone in the company, yet my only means of keeping Falconer at bay was to stick close to Mr. Pope's or to the theatre, where Falconer seemed reluctant to set foot. For the next week I saw no sign of that dread hooded figure, but this time I did not fool myself into thinking that he had gone away. I kept a vigilant watch, sometimes rising in the small hours of the night to gaze out at the moonlit lanes and hedgerows.

"Widge," Sander said one day on our way to the Globe. "We're friends, aren't we?"

"Aye," I said, and felt I spoke the truth.

"Then will you tell me please why you always glance about so nervously? You look like a dickey bird in a yard full of cats, as Mr. Pope would say."

"It's naught. I'm not used to the city yet, that's all." There was some truth in that, too. But it was also true that I no longer found the landscape of church spires and grimy tenements so strange. London speech no longer felt so foreign on my ear or on my tongue, and I'd learned to ignore the clamor of its streets.

"You know, five minutes' walk in that direction"—he pointed south—"brings you into the country. And tomorrow is our idle day."

The prospect of an afternoon in the fields and woods

was tempting—until I thought of Falconer. "I don't suppose you'd care to come along."

"I don't mind. I've nothing against the country."

To my relief, Julian agreed to join us. The larger the company, the safer I would be. I stopped short of inviting Nick, though. Not that he would have gone anyway. It was obvious that he no longer considered himself a prentice. He avoided our company, preferring to spend his time with his drinking companions, mostly hired men from the less reputable theatre companies. When forced to rub elbows with us boys, he put on superior airs.

That morning, during fencing instruction, Mr. Armin and Mr. Phillips were wanted downstairs, and Nick interpreted this to mean that he was in charge. "All right now, line up here and let's see what sort of scrimers you are."

"Take a walk in the Thames," Julian told him and turned away.

Nick stepped in front of him. "I said we'll see what you've learned. Would you prefer to demonstrate against the wall, or against me?"

Julian considered a moment. "Well, I'd say the wall has more wits."

"It's too bad you're not as quick with your sword as with your tongue. I think you've all been playing at girls too long. That's what you look like, with your mincing steps and your polite little cuts and thrusts. And you—" He gave Julian's stick a blow with his own. "You're the worst of the lot. You'd best stick to dancing."

Julian's face, always pale, had gone white, and his eyes narrowed. "I'll dance on your grave, you sot," he said, and came on guard.

Nick smiled nastily, as though this was what he had been waiting for. He brought his stick to high ward, seeming to invite a thrust from Julian. When it came, he stepped aside and struck Julian on the collarbone. Julian staggered, his face drawn with pain.

Nick stood calmly waiting for the next move. Julian feigned another *stocatta*, then performed one of the *passatas* we had practiced so interminably. His stick caught Nick beneath the breastbone. He let out a grunt of surprise and pain.

His mood changed suddenly. He set upon Julian like a Tom 'a Bedlam, striking edgeblows, downright blows, blows which had no name. "You'll hurt him!" I shouted and flung my stick at Nick's legs. It served only to anger him more. "Do something!" I told Sander.

Sander stepped forward with his stick raised. "Nick! Stop now!" He might as well have told the wall to stop standing there.

Being small, I had never been one to solve a problem by a physical attack. I preferred to talk my way out of things or to perform Cobbe's Traverse, that is to run. But Nick would not listen to reason, and running would only leave Julian to his fate. He had rescued me, and now he needed my help. My fencing skills were no match for Nick's, so I fell back on the method of defense that every child of the orphanage learns—catch-as-catch-can wrestling.

I at least had the advantage of surprise. I threw myself at Nick's legs, and all his weight collapsed on me. The first principle of wrestling is to hang on to your opponent come what may, so I clung to Nick's breeches like a leech, though he kicked madly and pummeled my back with his fists.

I felt his struggles suddenly grow more desperate and lifted my face to see why. Julian had his stick pressed against Nick's throat-bole. The more fiercely Nick struggled and clawed, the more pressure Julian applied, yet Nick refused to yield.

"That will do!" a voice rang out. "Let him up!"

Julian cautiously removed the stick, and I disentangled myself. Mr. Armin stood scowling at us, but under the mask of disapproval I detected a hint of amusement. I wondered how long he had stood observing before he interfered.

He offered a hand to Nick, who ignored it and got unsteadily to his feet, rubbing his windpipe and glaring at us like some trapped and wounded beast.

"If you're quite done trying to kill one another," Mr. Armin said, "we'll continue with our lessons. Not you, Nick," he added as Nick retrieved his singlestick. "They'll be wanting you downstairs, to rehearse *Love's Labour's.*"

"What part?" Nick growled, his voice sounding choked and weak.

"Dumaine."

Nick stared at him. "A man's part?"

"Do you imagine you can pass for a girl with that voice? It sounds as though Julian squeezed the last drop of sweetness from it."

Certainly there was no sweetness in the glance Nick threw us as he left the room.

"If Nick is to take on men's roles," Mr. Armin said, "that will change things for you boys as well. Sander, you and Julian will begin studying Nick's old roles. Widge, you'll be given some of Sander's duties, and his smaller parts. Can you manage that?"

"Yes, sir." I tried to sound confident.

He raised his eyebrows. "What happened to 'aye'?"

"I'm trying to civilize me speech—*my* speech."

He nodded thoughtfully. "A pity, though. Soon you'll sound the same as all the rest of us."

As we returned to our lessons, Julian said, "That was a brave thing you did."

I shrugged. "You were no coward yourself. I was afeard you'd thropple him."

"It'd be no more than he deserves."

"That's so, saying we fight like girls. I daresay 'a's never had a girl do such as that to him."

Julian gave me a curious look and seemed about to say something, but Mr. Armin interrupted. "We're not doing voice lessons, you two! Lay on!"

. . .

Our country outing next day was more in the nature of a rehearsal at first. Sander and Julian brought along the sides they needed in order to learn Nick's old roles. The brief bits I inherited were not worth the bother of a separate side. I merely jotted them down as Sander recited them.

Without thinking, I wrote them in Dr. Bright's charactery. Julian peered over my shoulder. "What sort of writing is *that*? I thought Mr. Shakespeare's hand was hard to read."

"Ah . . . it's just . . . something of me own invention." I tried to tuck the paper into my wallet, but Sander plucked it from my grasp.

"Let me see." He turned the paper this way and that, frowning. "Can you actually read this?"

"When it's right side up." I tried to retrieve the paper, but he kept it from me—an easy task, considering our relative heights.

"No, no. Wait a bit. This is amazing, you know. You can write out anything in this fashion?"

"Well, no," I lied. "It's rather slow going, in truth."

"Slow?" Julian said. "You wrote out those lines as quickly as Sander said them. A trick like that could be really useful. Why, you could copy down the plays of the Lord Admiral's men, word for word!"

"*Steal* them?" I said.

Julian shrugged. "They do it to us."

"That's because our plays are better than theirs," Sander said. "Not much point in our copying their weak stuff, is there?"

"I suppose not. All the same, there should be some use for that writing of yours, Widge. You should show it to Mr. Heminges."

"What?" I said, disguising my real dismay with mock dismay. "And saddle meself wi' yet another duty?"

Sander laughed. "He's right. We'll keep mum about it. Right, Julian?"

"I'm not one to give away others' secrets," Julian said.

The day was too fine to spend it all on lines. Goodwife Willingson had packed a cold meal for us, and we chose an inviting spot in the shade of an ancient oak. When I had had my fill, I stretched out and watched the clouds, as I had so often done in the meadows about Berwick.

"Look at him," Sander said. "He's in his element. We'll have to truss him up and carry him back to the city like a captured deer."

I turned my head to make some lazy reply, but it was stopped in my throat by the sight of a dark-clothed figure coming down the road. My face must have reflected my alarm, for Julian said, "What's wrong, Widge?"

"Someone's coming," I breathed.

The others turned to see who was approaching. "It's only Mr. Shakespeare," Julian said. I gave a sigh of relief. "Who did you think it was?"

"I was afeared it was—it was me master."

"He must be a harsh one, for you to fear him so."

"Aye. He is that." So pensive and self-absorbed was Mr. Shakespeare that he walked by without even noting our presence. "Should we not at least greet him?" I asked.

Julian shook his head. "Better not. If he's mulling over some problem in a play, he won't welcome the interruption."

"Why is 'a so glum and gloomy, do you think?"

Julian slid closer to me and said confidentially, "I've heard it said he's brooding on a thwarted love affair."

Sander gave him an indignant look. "The man has a wife and two daughters in Stratford."

Julian grinned. "When did that ever prevent a man from having a love affair?"

"You clod. If you want to know what I think, I think it's his son that's the cause of it."

"I didn't know he had a son."

"He doesn't, any longer. The boy grew ill and died while Mr. Shakespeare was here in London. I doubt that he's ever forgiven himself."

"Perhaps," I said, " 'a's simply ruled by a melancholy humour."

"A what?" said Sander.

"Me old master says we're all ruled by the four humours, and when we're ill or out of sorts, it's because we ha' too much of one. Now, Nick, 'a's choleric—hot and dry. Dr. Bright would prescribe something cold and wet, to offset it."

"All the beer he drinks doesn't seem to help much."

"Perhaps Julian had it right," I said. " 'A should take a walk in the Thames."

Julian laughed. "What would your master make of me?"

"Sanguine, I'd say."

"And me?" said Sander.

I considered a moment. "For you, they would ha' to think up a whole new category."

Sander aimed a good-natured swat at me, which I

dodged. He grabbed me, and laughing, we rolled about in the grass like two pups. "You're daft, the both of you," Julian said. Then, apparently feeling left out, he pulled up tufts of grass and flung them at us.

Sander spat out a few blades and whispered, "Let's get him!"

"Aye!" We sprang for Julian. He backed up against the tree, calling "No! No!" between fits of laughter. But when we took hold of his arms and tried to drag him down, he turned suddenly serious, indeed angry. "No! I don't want to wrestle!"

We teased him a moment longer, but he remained stiff and stern, so we left off. For some time afterward, a melancholy humour seemed to rule us as well. A gloominess was cast over our day, as though a cloud had come across the sun. But gradually we warmed to one another again and spent several hours poking about a stagnant pond and playing a game of nineholes with stones, and in other pursuits too trivial to recount. When we heard the bells in Southwark ringing vespers, we were reluctant to return—not just the country boy, I think, but all of us.

The week that followed was mostly uneventful, if days which begin with two hours of manual labor, proceed to four hours of lessons and rehearsals, and conclude with performing in or assisting with a different play each afternoon can be called uneventful. Compared to the preceding perilous weeks, this was a veritable holiday. I was not locked in any rooms, nor were any daggers held to my throat. I did not wander into any dangerous parts of the city, nor risk my life crossing the Thames.

Though I was never quite able to put Falconer out of my mind, I saw no sign of him. Surely, I thought, even he must have given up by now. I did not even quarrel with Nick, for he no longer took lessons with us mere prentices. He still played a few of his old parts, but most of the time he was downstairs, rehearsing men's roles.

Or at least he was supposed to be. In truth, he was still up to his old tricks, throwing his money away on dice and drink all night long, then coming to rehearsal half-drunk or late, or both. It was as though he had taken on a role he was not prepared to play, not only on stage but in life, and was looking for someone who would tell him what to do next. Yet, though he received advice from all quarters, he heeded none of it.

Before his second week was out, the part in *Love's Labour's* was given to Chris Beeston, and Nick was back upstairs with us, practicing his swordsmanship. "What he needs," Julian said, "is not fencing lessons but lessons in manners."

"Would you like to be the one to learn them to him?" I said.

Julian rolled his eyes. "And you could use a few lessons in grammar."

Nick's attitude toward us was even more hostile than before, especially toward Sander, who had taken over several of Nick's roles. With the demotion of Nick to our ranks, the peaceful interlude began to slip away, and my life once more became complicated, filled with anxiety and finally danger.

The first complication cropped up soon after Nick's return. The moment we arrived at the Globe that morning, we sensed that something was in the air. The sharers were in the property room, discussing some matter so intently that none of them so much as raised a hand to greet us. Halfway through the morning, we discovered what the matter was.

For a change, Nick was on time for fencing practice, and Mr. Armin was late. When he finally arrived, he beckoned to us, cleared his throat comically, and proclaimed with exaggerated formality, "Oyez, oyez! Be it known that the Lord Chamberlain's Men have been asked, or commanded if you will, to present the play *The Tragedy of Hamlet* at Whitehall a fortnight from this day!"

The other prentices looked at one another in surprise— or was it alarm? "What is Whitehall?" I whispered to Julian.

"The royal court."

"You mean the palace? Where the queen lives?"

"No," he said sarcastically, "the royal *tennis* court, you sot."

Two weeks seemed to me ample time to prepare, but the company behaved as though Judgment Day were almost upon them and they must put not only their parts but their entire lives in order. Our property men spent most of their day at the office of the queen's master of revels, preparing elaborate scenery for the great event, so the task of seeing to the properties for the regular performances fell to us prentices. It was not unusual in those next weeks for a player to cry "Behold!" and open the curtains of the rear alcove to reveal two frantic prentices struggling with some unwieldy piece of scenery or furniture. Our tire man, too, deserted us, leaving us to clean our costumes and hold our split seams together as best we might.

The principal players, meantime, rehearsed *Hamlet* endlessly, employing a slightly different version each day, as Mr. Shakespeare deleted or added passages to suit the fancy of the master of revels.

Even Julian and Sander, who ordinarily took things as they came, seemed to breathe in the air of anxiety that hung about the place. "Why is everyone in such a dither?" I asked Julian. "You've played at the court before, ha' you not?"

"Not I. The company has, many times. But this time is different. I don't know quite all that's behind it, but I do know the company got on Her Majesty's bad side a few months ago by giving a private performance of *Richard III* for the earl of Essex."

"What's wrong in that?"

"The queen had said that no one should perform the play, because it shows a ruler being deposed. I suppose she didn't want it giving anyone any ideas. But apparently that's just what Essex meant to do, for the day after the performance, he tried to gather an army to storm the palace."

"What happened?"

Julian shrugged. "She made him king." He let me puzzle over that a moment, then laughed. "He didn't succeed, of course, you ninny. The queen's guard threw him in the Tower, and a few days later they chopped off his head. Because of the play, the queen suspected our players of being in league with Essex. They weren't, of course. But they're all walking very carefully now, to avoid treading on the queen's toes."

"I can see why," I said. "If Essex was the queen's favorite and she chopped his costard off, who kens what she might do to someone she doesn't care for?"

Julian nodded soberly, as thought contemplating what dreadful fate the queen might devise if she were truly displeased.

Our lessons were all but suspended for a time, but Mr. Armin insisted on an hour's fencing practice each day. We worked frequently with blunted rapiers and protective plates. We were even permitted one day to strap on a bag of sheep's blood, which gave an added luster to our mock death throes.

Nick and Julian were again paired. Julian wore the protective plate and the bladder of blood. Nick wielded a blunted rapier. He was having trouble piercing the blood bag with the dull point and, growing angry, he thrust harder than was necessary and without the necessary control. His point struck the bag high and, deflected by the metal plate, caught Julian squarely in the center of the chest.

Julian gave a sharp gasp and went down on one knee, holding his chest and biting his lip against the pain. Sander laughed, obviously thinking it was all a sham. "Good acting!"

"He's not acting." Mr. Armin strode over to Julian. "What is it? What's happened?"

Nick stood white-faced, his sword hanging at his side. "I—it was an accident. I—I stuck him—"

Mr. Armin supported Julian with one arm and helped him sit on the floor. "Let me see," he said, and began unhooking the front of Julian's doublet.

"No, no," Julian protested. "It's nothing." But his strained voice and drawn face gave the lie to this.

"I'll decide that," Mr. Armin said.

"I didn't mean to do it," Nick put in, sullenly. When Mr. Armin ignored him, he turned away and began pacing irritably back and forth.

Mr. Armin tried to pull open the doublet, but Julian pushed his hand away and struggled to rise. "I'm all right, I tell you."

"Stop fighting me. This is not time for false pride or false courage." When Mr. Armin yanked the doublet open, I could see the red stain on Julian's linen shirt. "You see, you're bleeding." He drew out the kerchief from his sleeve.

"Please," Julian begged, pulling at the gaping front of his doublet. "I'll see to it myself."

"Yes, and bleed to death by yourself, most like." Mr. Armin forced Julian's hands away and pulled at the neck of the shirt, laying Julian's torso bare.

In truth, though, it was not bare. A cloth was wound tightly about his chest. "What is this?" Mr. Armin demanded. Then his puzzled scowl transformed into a look of disbelief. "The devil take me!" he breathed.

Julian was fairly frantic now, clutching at the front of his shirt, while tears streamed down his cheeks. "Let me alone! Please, let me alone!"

Mr. Armin recovered and shook his head. "We have to stop the bleeding. Just let me put this on the wound, and you can hold it in place. All right?"

Julian nodded shortly and turned his head aside in an attempt to hide his tears. Sharing his embarrassment, we hung our heads and moved back a few paces.

"Come, now." Mr. Armin lifted Julian's slight body easily in his arms. "We'll get you downstairs where you can lie down, and then we'll find someone who can bandage that properly."

"But why—?" Nick started to ask. Mr. Armin shot him a warning glance, and carried Julian from the room.

When they were gone, Nick said, "Why can't he bandage it himself? Surely it's not so bad as to require a doctor. Though from the way the boy carried on, you'd think I'd gutted him. It couldn't be that bad. Could it?"

I glanced at Sander and knew from the stunned look on his face that, like me, he had guessed the truth that Nick was either too slow-witted or too unobservant to see. "I don't believe the wound is what concerns Mr. Armin, or Julian," Sander said.

"What, then?"

Sander looked to me and shrugged. "It may as well be said. It'll be no secret soon."

I shook my head. "I'll not be the one to tell it."

"Tell *what*?" Nick demanded.

Sander gave a sigh of resignation. "It would seem," he said, "that Julian is a girl."

I had rarely seen Nick at a loss for words, but he was now. He gaped at us, then at the door through which Julian had been carried. "A girl," he said finally, as though unsure of the meaning of the word. "That's impossible."

Certainly it seemed impossible that such a fact could have escaped our notice all this time. But of course, looking backward, I could see a dozen clues that, had I bothered to add them together, would have led me to that very conclusion.

"Impossible or not," Sander said, "I'm afraid it's true."

Nick's astonishment gave way to anger. "It can't be true! You can't tell me I've been fencing with a girl for most of a year, and never knew it!"

"I won't tell you, then, but it's so all the same."

Nick stalked back and forth, scowling and slicing the air with his blade, as though to fend off the truth that was attempting to seize him. At last he cried, "God's blood! A girl!" and, flinging the sword aside, stormed out of the room.

Sander clucked his tongue in sympathy. "It's a hard morsel for him to swallow. But even harder for Julian. They'll never let him go on performing."

"*Her*," I reminded him.

"Yes," he said. "Her."

Mr. Phillips's wife was sent for to bandage the wound, which was not so grave, aside from the damage it had done to Julian's pride and to her future as a player. Julia, I should now call her, for that was her given name.

Mistress Phillips tried to coax Julia to come home with her, but Julia refused. "I have never yet missed a performance, and I do not intend to miss this one."

After much discussion, the sharers concluded that it was better to let a girl play the part than to assign it to a prentice who would have to read the lines from a side.

Besides, it began to look as though one of us might be needed to take Nick's place. He had left the theatre and not returned, and there was little more than an hour until performance. "We could go seek him out," Sander suggested to Mr. Heminges. "No doubt we'll find him in his usual haunts."

"M-meaning an ale house," Mr. Heminges said sourly. "Perhaps you'd b-best do that. Just be sure the t-two of you are b-back in time, else I'll be out there m-myself, clean-shaven and speaking f-falsetto."

Despite the circumstances, we could not help laughing at the picture this conjured up. "You may well laugh," Mr. Heminges said, "but I served my t-time in skirts, and by all accounts I was quite f-fetching. More so than N-Nick, certainly. But though Nick may not be fetching, still he must be f-fetched."

"And though 'a be not comely, yet 'a must come," I added, drawing an appreciative laugh from the others.

"Very good, Widge," said Mr. Heminges. "You've the wit of a true p-player."

As Sander and I walked toward the river, I said, "Do you think that I could actually be a player?"

He gave me a puzzled look. "You say that as though the idea had just struck you. Isn't that what you came here for?"

"Oh. Aye, of course it is." Once again, I was sorely tempted to tell him the truth. I was weary of carrying the baggage of that secret about with me, always having to be careful not to let it slip. I tried to imagine how Julia must have felt, guarding her secret for years, wanting so badly to belong to the company of players that she would risk such a desperate device and yet, because of that very device, never being able to truly belong.

We were, as she had said, birds of a feather, for I had never belonged anywhere, either. Now there was a chance that I might, and I could not bring myself to endanger that chance by revealing my original purpose here, even though I had abandoned that purpose and, to all appearances, so had Falconer.

The south bank of the Thames was like a poor reflection of the north bank, a sort of lesser London. Across the river the great houses of great gentlemen lined the embankment. Here on the lower ground the buildings were nearly as imposing in size but housed a separate family behind each of their many grimy windows. Scattered among these tenements were smaller dwellings that had given over their ground floors to some business, usually a tavern.

"How in heaven's name will we ken which one Nick is in?"

"Any which looks prosperous or reputable," Sander said, "we can surely pass by."

We found him in a place with a sagging roof and the customary ivy growing up the front wall. Nick sat at one of the stained, scarred tables, in the company of two fellows I took to be university students, a species we all knew well, as they had more money and leisure for playgoing than the working class.

Sander and I stood just inside the door and tried to attract Nick's attention, but he was too absorbed in his ale, or had absorbed too much of it, to notice. Finally we approached his table. "Nick," Sander said.

Nick glanced up. "What are you doing here? They don't serve boys."

"Oh, they serve them occasionally," one of the students put in. "Well roasted, with an apple in their mouth."

Nick laughed harder than the jest deserved. Sander said, "They're wanting you back at the Globe. It's nearly performance time."

"I don't need you to tell me that. I'll be along—when it suits me."

"I thought you'd want to know, too, that Julian isn't badly hurt."

"What's this?" the student said eagerly. "You've been dueling?"

"A trifle," Nick said with a pale smile, then turned on us. "Out of here with you now, before I give the same to you, and worse!"

Sander backed away. "I just thought perhaps you were . . . well, reluctant to come back and face her." I could tell as soon as the final word left his mouth that he would have liked to call it back. But the student had already seized upon it.

"*Her?*" he echoed, laughing. "Don't tell me you've taken to fighting women, Nick?"

Nick clapped his mug on the table so fiercely that it cracked the earthenware. "I take that as an insult!"

"Take it however you like," the student said casually. "It was offered as a jest, nothing more." He gave his companion a sidelong glance of amusement. "Unless of course it's true."

Nick got unsteadily to his feet and reached across to tap the student on the front of his embroidered doublet. "Be careful what you say, or I'll show you that steel is true."

"Quite a boast for a man without a sword," the student said.

"Swords are easily come by, as are university asses."

The student leaped up to face him, knocking his chair to the floor. "Your jest has the bitter taste of an insult!"

"Here now, here now!" the tavern keeper called. "No quarreling inside! Take your dispute into the street!"

Sander snatched at Nick's sleeve. "Let's go, Nick, before it comes to blows."

Nick pushed him away. "I've no fear of blows. They're braver than words." But I could see how his hand trembled.

"No more do I fear them," the student replied, though his face had gone white as *Hamlet*'s ghost.

"I'll give you cause to, then!" Nick raised a hand as if to strike the other.

The student's hand went to the hilt of his rapier. "I am no woman, to be silenced with a slap!"

This was more than Nick's pride could bear. He lunged across the table, seized the weapon of the second student, and yanked it free of its hanger. "Enough of words!"

The student sprang away from the table and drew his sword as well. The tavern keeper shouted a curse, and Sander called out, "No!" but both protests were lost in the sudden clash of steel upon steel.

It was obvious at once that Nick was overmatched, and I believe he recognized it. The look on his face was that of a man who has stepped into a stream and found that the water is over his head.

He beat away the student's first two blows, but the third stung his leg and made him shuffle backward. The student followed step for step, like his partner in a deadly dance.

All the techniques Nick had learned at Mr. Armin's hands seemed to desert him. He hardly tried to strike an offensive blow; it was all he could do to ward off those of his opponent. In desperation, he drew his dagger and held it before him as an added defense. The student did the same.

As much as I disliked Nick, I felt something like sympathy for him. Though he was no friend, yet he was a fellow prentice, and I had no desire to see him run through. "What will we do?" I asked Sander above the din.

He shook his head despondently. "There's nothing we can do. It's a matter of honor."

"Honor? 'A'll be spitted like a pigeon an we don't help him. Where's the honor in that?"

"It's his fight, not ours."

"Then I'll make it ours!" I hoisted a three-legged stool, meaning to launch it at Nick's opponent. Before I could, the student moved in and feinted an edge blow at Nick's legs. When Nick lowered his dagger to ward it, the student delivered a quick *stocatta* to Nick's throat.

Nick gave a strangled cry and staggered backward. Both his weapons fell from his grasp as he clutched at the wound. He collided with a bench and toppled to the floor.

"The devil take you!" I shouted at the student. "You've killed him!"

22

I let fly with the stool. It knocked the student's rapier from his hand and struck him on the shoulder. Without waiting to see what he would do, I knelt beside Nick and pulled his hands away from the wound. It was a serious one, but the knowledge of medicine and anatomy I'd absorbed willy-nilly in Dr. Bright's service told me that no artery had been severed. The thrust had struck next to his throat-bole and been stopped by his jaw. Still, there was a copious flow of blood. Using Nick's dagger, I cut off the sleeve of his linen shirt and pressed it into a ball over the wound.

Nick's eyes were wide, darting about as though searching for something. He tried to rise, and I put a knee on his chest. "Lie still, now. We've got to stop the bleeding."

When the first compress was dyed red, I had Sander cut another and pressed it to the wound until at last the bleeding slowed enough to allow me to bind it in place.

"Stay there a bit, yet," I told Nick. When I rose and looked about, the two students were gone.

"How bad is he?" Sander asked, his voice anxious and unsteady.

" 'A'll live, most like. What do we do wi' him now?"

"The tavern keeper's sent for a constable—which is why those two fled. You can go to prison for dueling."

"That doesn't seem to keep anyone from it."

"No. Some men's honor is easily insulted."

"Not mine," I said. "There's little in this world worth fighting over, as far as I can see."

"Then why did you take Nick's part?"

"Did you not once say he was a part of the family?"

"So I did. All the same, it was a brave thing."

I shrugged. " 'A'd have done as much for me."

Sander looked down at Nick, who lay staring at the rotted ceiling. "I doubt it."

The authorities seemed to feel that Nick had suffered enough. Instead of taking him to prison, they took him to a hospital. Within a fortnight, he was on his feet again—too late to be of any use in our command performance at Whitehall.

We could have dealt with his absence alone, for Sander had been studying the part of Hamlet's mother, but we were deprived of our Ophelia as well. Had the decision been left to Julia, I feel sure she would have taken the risk, for she had gone on playing her old roles on the stage of the Globe, despite the fact that her secret was out. Though I didn't expect anyone would deliberately give her away, someone might let the truth slip, as Sander himself had done at the tavern.

I knew that, were my own secret revealed, I would not have had the nerve to face Mr. Pope or Mr. Heminges or Mr. Shakespeare or Sander. Julia was the only one I felt might understand. Yet I wasn't sure. When I believed her to be a boy, I had begun to think of her as a friend. Now suddenly I felt as though she were a stranger. Before, I had talked freely with her, more freely than I ever had with anyone, even Sander. Now, when we were thrown together, I scarcely knew what to say.

During a performance of *A Larum for London* I was assisting in the tiring-room when she came into the room to change costume. "You don't mind if I forgo your help, do you?" she said dryly.

"No, no," I said, embarrassed. She disappeared into the wardrobe. It took me some time to think of how best to ask what I wanted to ask her. Finally, concluding that there was no good way, I said it straight out. "Why did you do it?"

After a long pause, her voice came from the other room. "Do what?"

"You ken."

She emerged, still hooking her bodice together. "Disguise myself?" She shrugged. "For the same reason we all do it. To give others what they expect of us."

"I don't ken what you mean."

"Yes, you do. You do the same yourself."

"Disguise meself?"

"Of course. Why do you speak so politely to Mr. Armin and Mr. Pope and the other sharers, and do as they tell you without complaint?"

I laughed. "Because they'd box me ears an I did not."

"I doubt that. Anyway, you don't act that way with Sander and me."

"You'd think me daft an I did."

"You see? We play the roles others expect of us. If I'd come here as a girl and said I wished to be a player, they'd have laughed and turned me away. Girls are not permitted on the stage; it corrupts them." She shook her head and smiled bitterly. "If I was not corrupted long since, growing up in Alsatia among thieves and beggars, then I must be incorruptible." She hoisted herself up on the table next to me so casually that I had to remind myself that this was no boy made up to resemble a girl, but the actual thing.

"It was nothing new to me," she went on, "dressing and acting as a boy does. My da wanted a boy, and made no secret of it—to carry on the family trade, you might say. He didn't provide me with much girl's clothing. 'You can't outrun the law wearing skirts,' he always said." She laughed and flapped the hem of her elegant costume. "In truth, I wore skirts and bodices regularly only after I began masquerading as a boy."

"Will they let you go on wi' it?"

Her face grew solemn, and she shook her head. "They can't, now that they know. If the queen gets wind of it, we're all in the soup."

"What will you do, then?"

"Would that I knew," she said, with something nearer to despair than I had ever heard from her. "I've never wanted anything but to be a player, ever since the day I crept into the theatre at Blackfriars and watched *The Lady of May* through the crack of the door." She stared into space, as though seeing that performance once more. A tear welled in her eye and coursed down her rouged cheek. She raised a sleeve to dash it impatiently away and forced a smile. "Perhaps I'll take up my da's trade after all. As I said, it's best to be what people expect of you."

"It's not fair," I said.

"No," she said. "It's not." She jumped down from the table. "I'll miss my cue."

"Does it matter, now?"

She shrugged and gave an ironic smile. "It does to me."

Of course what she said was perfectly true. The company could not let her go on performing for long. No matter how loyal or how closemouthed the other players were, sooner or later someone was sure to let the truth slip out, and this time the company might not be let off lightly as they had been in the Essex affair.

Even if we could have carried the deceit off successfully at the Globe, we dared not risk it under the very nose of the queen. The part of Ophelia would have to go to a boy. Sander was out of the question, being occupied with Nick's part. Sam and James, the hopefuls, were neither old enough nor experienced enough.

So the company was left with a clear choice: either they must hire a boy from some other company, someone who would be unfamiliar with the role and with the methods of the Chamberlain's Men, or they must settle for me.

They settled for me.

To the company's credit, they did not simply thrust the part upon me. Mr. Heminges asked me if I wanted it. I was not used to being asked my opinion on anything, and it confused me. Did I truly have a choice, or was this an offer, like Simon Bass's offer, that I was not permitted to refuse? "I don't suppose I could think on it."

"We have less than a w-week left until the p-performance."

"Aye," I said mournfully. "I ken that."

"Julia has offered to g-go over the p-part with you."

"That would help," I admitted. "But I'm just not certain. I mean, do you really think I'm ready to play so important a role? Before so important an audience?"

"If we didn't feel you c-could do it, we would not have offered it to you. Whether or n-no you have the ability is not the question, but whether or n-not you have the c-courage."

If this was calculated to prick my pride, it worked, and that surprised me. I was sure that what small pride I had was buried deep, for it seldom bothered me. I had never been much of a hand for courage, either. When two paths were open to me—which is not often in the life of a prentice—I took the one easiest to travel, without regard to where it led. I had never deliberately chosen the perilous or demanding path.

But I had done many things recently that I had never done before, and never dreamed I would do. "Well," I said with a sigh, "I suppose if Julian could be a boy for three years, I can be a girl for an hour or two."

Without Julia's help, I could never have hoped to be ready. Each afternoon, long after the others had gone, we sat and went over the lines again and again. She taught me not only the words but their proper reading and what gestures to use. As difficult as this was for me, it must have been doubly difficult for her, having to tutor me in a role she had worked so hard to make her own, a role she had gone through years of disguise and deception to be able to play.

And here was I, with no real notion of being a player until a few weeks before, having the part handed to me. Yet she made no complaint. In fact, she was so generous as to tell me that, if she had to surrender the part to someone, she was glad it was me. I feel sure, though, that her cheerful acceptance was itself a disguise. Something in her eyes spoke of sorrow, and in unguarded moments they sometimes shone with tears. I determined then to put every ounce of effort and ability I had into playing the part, so that she would not be disappointed in me.

I had no time for a prentice's lessons, or a prentice's tasks. Every available moment was spent rehearsing, sometimes under the eye of Mr. Shakespeare or Mr. Phillips, who pointed out my many flaws. For an hour or two each day, I worked with the other players. Only twice did I share the stage with our Hamlet, Mr. Burbage, and then only to work out where I was to move and on what line. He was patient enough with me and my blunders, but he seldom displayed any real warmth or friendliness.

That week was a paradoxical one. Because I trod the same ground over and over, repeating my lines until they threatened to choke me, each day seemed endless. Yet taken as a whole, the week passed with astounding speed. On Wednesday evening, we ferried across the river to rehearse before the queen's master of revels. The performance was a nightmare.

The stage was half the size of the Globe's, which drove us to distraction. To add to the confusion, there were all the new properties and painted backdrops our hired men had constructed. Whatever way I turned, I came up against another player or a piece of scenery. My lines, which were not yet securely seated in my brain, flew from it like startled birds.

To our tiny audience, it must have looked as though we were playing not *The Tragedy of Hamlet* but *The Comedy of Errors*. When at long last we came to the end of it, I had made up my mind that my best course would be to share Ophelia's fate—that is, to throw myself over the side of the wherryboat into the Thames and join the rest of the offal there, none of which could be any more putrid than my performance had been.

No one else seemed upset, either with the rehearsal or with my part in it. "You needn't look so glum, Widge," Mr. Armin said. "A bad rehearsal means a good performance."

"That makes no sense at all. You may as well say a bad cook makes a good meal."

He laughed. "It's true, though. You'll see. Besides, we still have three days before the performance."

I tried to take some hope from this, but secretly I was wondering how far I could get from London in three days.

Saturday dawned grey and gloomy, in keeping with my mood. Julia and Sander tried to cheer me, but the only thing that might have done the trick was to hear that the queen had changed her mind and would have the Lord Admiral's men instead.

Immediately after the performance of *Satiromastix*, the company set out for Whitehall, on a barge provided by Her Majesty—a gesture not unlike providing the cart to haul a condemned man to the scaffold.

Julia was asked to come along and assist behind the

scenes, on the condition that she dress as a girl. She refused. But as we were climbing onto the barge, she came running down the landing stairs, clothed in her costume from *Love's Labour's Lost*, her skirts lifted so high we could see her ankles. She sprang onto the barge and took a place on the railing next to me, flushed and scant of breath and—something I had somehow failed to notice before— quite pretty.

"I'm glad you decided to come," I said. "I can do wi' a bit of support."

She shrugged casually. "You'll be all right without me. Actually I came along in order to meet the queen."

"You lie," I said, and she laughed.

I had always thought of Whitehall as being just that—a large hall, painted white. But what lay before us was more in the nature of a small, walled town. I gawked about me like the greenest country lad as we were escorted to a massive square hall with a lead roof and high, arched windows. Within, the hall was as grand as the grandest cathedral.

"Where is the stage?" I asked Sander.

"There is none. Only the floor."

"Gog's malt!" I murmured. We would not be set apart from our distinguished audience at all; instead, we would be playing practically in their royal laps.

It was fortunate that my entrance came well into the play, for I spent the first quarter hour of the performance in the jakes, emptying my stomach of what little supper I had been able to force down. Julia found me there and pulled me like a balky sheep to the stage entrance. "Wait! Wait!" I whispered urgently.

"What is it?"

"I can't recall me first line!"

"Do you doubt that?" she said.

"What?"

"That's your line, Widge. 'Do you doubt that?' "

"Oh." The cue line came to my ears. Chris Beeston took me by the arm and strode onto the stage with me in tow. Ah, well, I told myself, there's no turning back now.

Sometimes in dreams we do things we could never do in everyday life. The moment I stood before that glittering crowd of sumptuously dressed courtiers, I lapsed into a sort of dream. Through some miraculous process, I ceased to be Widge and became Ophelia, except for some small part of myself that seemed to hover overhead, observing my transformation with amazement.

The lines flowed from me as though they had just occurred to my brain and not been penned by Mr. Shakespeare a year earlier. The audience seemed vague and distant. Only when I had spoken my final line in the scene and swept off the stage did I come to myself again, to find Julia grasping my hands and fairly jumping up and down with delight. "You were wonderful! You didn't miss a single word!"

I grinned back at her. "I did so. I forgot to say 'So please you' to Polonius."

She gave me an exasperated shove. "You sot. Admit it; you were good, very good."

I shrugged, embarrassed. "An I was, I owe it to you. I'm only sorry you couldn't do the part yourself."

Her gaze fell. "It can't be helped." Then she put on something of a smile again and pulled at my wig. "You're all askew. Come sit down, I'll repair you."

So in the end it was not courage that got me through; it was a trick of the mind. As I had survived my orphanage days by pretending I was someone else, someone whose parents still lived and were great and wealthy and would someday come for him, so I survived my hour or so upon the stage by pretending I was a wistful Danish girl, driven mad by love.

After the play, we were presented to the queen and her court, and I was compelled to be Widge again. "What do I say?" I whispered to Sander as we stood in line like soldiers awaiting inspection—or execution.

"Don't say anything," Sander advised me. "Just smile and bow, and kiss her hand."

I practiced my smile. It felt as though I had painted it on, and the paint was cracking. By the time the queen approached, my dry lips were stuck so fast to my teeth that I feared if I pressed my mouth to her hand, I would draw blood.

Mr. Heminges introduced each member of the company in turn. Even had I not known the queen's countenance from the likeness of her that hung in every inn and shop, I could not have mistaken her. Among all those elegant lords and ladies, she was the most elegant of all, in her bearing and in her appearance. She looked far too young and sprightly to have worn the crown for over forty years.

Or so I thought, seeing her at a distance. When she stood before me, her face not three feet from mine, I saw that the fair complexion was a layer of white paint, a ghastly mask, through which her age clearly showed, and the red hair the result of dye. When she smiled, her teeth were black with decay.

"This is our Ophelia," Mr. Heminges was saying. "Widge has been with us but a few months."

I bowed quickly, as much to hide my shock as to do homage to her. She held out her gloved hand, and I touched my lips to it. Now I thought, she will move on. But to my horror, she spoke to me. "What sort of name is that?"

Pretend you're someone else, I told myself—someone charming and witty, someone whose voice works. "It's a— a sort of nickname, Your Majesty," I said, and the voice certainly sounded like someone else's.

"What is your Christian name, then?" She spoke with kindness and, it seemed, genuine interest.

"I don't ken. It's the only name I've got."

"Well, Widge, if you go on performing as admirably as you did for us, you'll make a name for yourself."

"Thank you, mum—I mean, Your Majesty." I bowed again, and when I came erect, she had moved on.

That night in bed, the evening's events replayed themselves over and over in my head. In the space of a few hours, I had done more than transform temporarily into Ophelia. I had undergone a more dramatic change, from a shabby impostor, a thief and orphan who had been given a task far beyond his abilities, into a reliable, valued member of an acting company who performed daily at the center of the universe.

The queen herself had said I would make a name for myself. A name? Yes, I needed a real name. I would not be plain Widge any longer. I would be . . . Pedringano. I said it aloud, grandly. "Pedringano!"

Sander stirred next to me. "What?"

"My name," I said, "is Pedringano!"

He hit me with a pillow. "Go to sleep, Widge. We have to haul scenery first thing in the morning."

Though the company had survived the command performance, our troubles were far from over. We were still desperately short of bodies to fill roles. When Julia gave up the role of Ophelia, she seemed to give up as well all hope of being a player.

Mr. Heminges offered her a position gathering money at one of the theatre entrances. Though I knew he meant well, Julia behaved as though she'd been offered a job as a dung collector. I understood her feelings, the more so because I'd now succumbed myself to what Mr. Pope called "the siren call."

The position of gatherer paid well, and carried a certain amount of responsibility, but it was not the same as being a player. Still, Julia admitted that she would have to make a living somehow. She stuck with it for one week.

From the stage, I could see her standing just inside the second-level entrance, her shoulders sagging under the weight of the money box, her eyes fixed on the stage, saying silently that she would give any amount of money to be up there with us. I would have given mine as well, had I had any.

When Monday's performance came around, she was not in her place. Mr. Phillips said that she had disappeared sometime during the night, taking the few articles of woman's clothing she owned, and leaving behind all her boy's garb.

I tried to understand that, too, but it was difficult. I had been persuaded that she and I were friends, and though I knew little as yet about what friendship entailed, I felt that surely a friend would wish to say farewell.

Nick seemed to have deserted us, too. Though some of the players had seen him up and about and looking well enough, save for a bandage on his throat, he did not return to the theatre. Sander went on substituting for him in *Hamlet*, and I for Julia, but the two of us could not hope to fill all the roles both of them had been playing.

A hired boy took on a few, and Chris Beeston reluctantly agreed to don women's costume again, and for a time the sharers scheduled the plays with the fewest female roles. But these were only temporary measures. If Nick did not rejoin us soon, a replacement would have to be found. Sander and I were dispatched once again to try and surprise him at one of his customary watering holes.

I doubted that he would show his face again at the tavern where he had fought the duel, and I was right. The only sign of Nick there was the blood stain he had left on the floorboards. We stopped at three other taverns before we finally discovered him at the sign of the Dagger, and then I had cause to wish we had not.

As soon as we stepped inside the door, Sander spotted him. "There he is, with a pot of ale in his hand as usual."

My eyes had not quite grown used to the dim interior. "Where?" Sander pointed. Nick sat at the far side of the room, gripping a pewter pot as if it were the only stable thing in the room. Across from him sat another familiar figure. His upper body was bent forward, as though to discuss some private matter. His face was shrouded in a dark hood, leaving only a hooked nose and a black, curly beard by which to identify him.

"Gog's blood!" I breathed. I backed through the door as noiselessly as I could and ducked into a narrow space between the tavern and the building next to it. There I stood, pressed to the wall, trying to recover my breath, which seemed to have been squeezed from my chest.

After a moment, Sander came into view, looking about in a bewildered fashion. "Whist!" I called softly. "Over here!" He turned in my direction. "No! Don't look at me!" I cried, and he turned away again, more bewildered than ever. "Is anyone coming out of the tavern?"

He glanced toward the door. "No."

Fearfully, I emerged from my hiding place and pulled at his arm. "Let's go."

"Where?"

"Back to the theatre."

"But—but what about Nick?"

"I'll explain later. Just come."

Good friend that he was, he did not waste time arguing. But when we had put several blocks behind us, he said, "Could you explain, now?"

How could I? What could I tell him? Would I be a better friend if I revealed the truth to him, or if I concocted another lie? Once again, two paths had opened before me, and I could take the expedient one, or the one that required courage.

"That man wi' Nick," I said. "I ken him."

"From the way you bolted, I'd guess you're not on the best of terms."

I couldn't help smiling grimly at this understatement. "You might say so." I paused, still considering the other path, then sighed and went on. " 'A's called Falconer. 'A's been sent here by Simon Bass to steal the book of *Hamlet*."

"Bass? The same Simon Bass who was with the Chamberlain's Men?"

"Aye, the very same." I knew what his next question would be, and I dreaded it.

"What has that to do with you?"

"I . . . I was sent wi' him. To copy the play."

Sander stared at me, his face a very picture of astonishment. "Copy it? How do you mean?"

"In the writing I showed you," I said, unable to meet his eyes.

"The devil take me!" He walked on in silence for a bit, trying, I guessed, to come to terms with this idea. "Have you done it?" he asked finally.

"Of course not! I made up me mind not to, long ago! Well, some time ago, anyway."

He shook his head in disbelief. "What a dunce I've been! I truly believed you wanted to be a player!"

"I do, Sander! As God's me witness, I do now!" He stared at me, and the look of mistrust in his eyes, where I had never seen it, pained me deeply. "I didn't think of it as wrong at first. I thought of it only as a job given me by me master. That was before I kenned any of you. Don't you see, an I'd meant to carry it out, I had ample chance. Gog's bread, I had the book in me hands!"

He blinked thoughtfully. "That's so," he admitted. But the look of mistrust lingered. "All the same, you made fools of us. You and Julia."

"I'm sorry." The words felt strange and foreign upon my tongue. It felt strange, too, to have told the harsh truth for once, rather than an easy lie, yet I did not regret it. "You won't tell the others?"

"How can I not? If that fellow is still planning to steal the book, they need to know."

" 'A won't come near the Globe himself. 'A's too canny for that."

"Then how—" He paused as the answer came to him. "You don't think Nick would—?"

"Aye. I've no doubt of it. An Falconer offers him enough money, 'a'll recite every line 'a recalls, and make up what 'a doesn't, and we've no way of preventing him."

"We could tell the sharers."

"And what good would that do? They can't stop him, either, short of locking him up, or cutting out his tongue. All it will do is bring out me own part in this matter."

"I suppose so." Sander shook his head. "I can't believe that Nick would really betray the company," he said, though the look on his face said that he found the idea all too likely. "But then," he added, "I'd never have believed it of you, either."

The fact that I had elected to tell the truth one time did not diminish my ability to lie accurately when the occasion demanded it. Upon our return, I told Mr. Heminges that we had failed to find Nick. For a moment, I feared that Sander might contradict me, but he let it go. That, I assumed, would be the end of the matter. Nick and Falconer would come to some mutually satisfactory agreement, and with any luck, we would never see either of them again.

Knowing Falconer as I did, I should have known better. I should have realized that he would not be content to take to Simon Bass a secondhand version of the play.

The following afternoon, we were performing *Tamburlaine*. I was playing several small roles, my most dramatic being that of a soldier who dies a bloody death in one of the battle scenes. I had just finished strapping on my blood bag and rapier and dressing myself and was about to step from the tiring-room, when the rear door of the theatre opened and Nick stepped inside. He let the door close softly behind him and stood gazing about, as if to see whether anything had changed in his absence.

I ducked back into the tiring-room, my mind in confusion. How could he have the nerve to come here, after selling us out to Falconer? Then, for the first time, it occurred to me that perhaps he had not. Perhaps he had refused Falconer's offer. Or perhaps there had been no such offer. What if, instead, Falconer had hired Nick to bring me to him? Or what if I had misjudged Nick altogether? What if, in spite of everything, he still felt some loyalty to his theatre family and, learning of my association with Falconer, he had come to expose me?

I stood against the wall for several long minutes, overcome with anxiety and indecision. The reflection staring back at me from the looking glass appeared grotesque and strange. What was I doing dressed in soldier's garb, with an oversized sword dragging the floor at my side? What had ever made me imagine that I could impersonate someone else, that I could be anything other than Widge, the orphan, the unwilling prentice of some unsympathetic master in some unbearable trade?

My heart sank, and I turned from the glass. I did not have the courage Julian had. If Nick was here to reveal my secret, I could not bear to witness it. I moved to the tiring-room door and peered out. To my surprise, Nick was gone. If I meant to make good my escape, now was the moment.

I slipped across the area behind the stage to the rear door without attracting anyone's attention. In another moment I would have been out of the theatre had not my notice been attracted by something out of the ordinary. The door of the property room, which always stood open during performances to give the players quick access to their properties, was now firmly closed. In the perpetual gloom that prevailed behind the stage, I could see a faint light issuing through the crack at the bottom of the door.

I hesitated. Was Nick within, searching for the book? Or was it some member of the company—Mr. Heminges, perhaps, seeking a moment of solitude in which to balance his accounts? A faint grating noise came from within the room, and it was not, I was certain, the sound of someone writing in a ledger.

Knowing full well that I might be sorry, I stepped away from the exit. Carefully lifting the latch on the property room door, I eased it open.

Inside, in the light of a candle, I could make out a figure crouched over one of the property trunks, lifting some object from it. As the figure stood and turned to the light, I saw that it was Nick, and that the object he held was a play book.

Before I could retreat from the doorway, Nick lifted his gaze and spied me. His hand went to his rapier, and he drew it from its hanger in one swift motion. "Hold!" he commanded, his voice as faint and rasping as the sound I had heard moments before—the sound of the trunk being forced open.

I could likely have pulled the door closed before his sword point reached me, but I did not. If I ran, even to bring help, I would be letting Nick go, and the play book with him, and betraying the company as surely as if I had taken it myself.

He beckoned with his blade. "Inside! And keep quiet!" I did as he said, but when he gestured for me to move to the rear of the room, I shook my head.

"I won't let you leave wi' that," I said in a voice nearly as faint and faltering as his.

"You can't stop me, Horse."

"I can call for help."

"I'll gut you if you do."

"I don't think so," I said, trying to sound confident. "If it hadn't been for me, you'd have bled to death on that tavern floor."

I had not expected his gratitude, but neither did I expect the response he gave. He shrugged contemptuously, as if to say he would as soon have been left to die. "No matter. Step aside."

"Nay," I said, gambling that he would not strike me. "Leave the book and go."

"Stand aside!" His voice broke like glass under the strain. His face reddened with anger and shame, and he swung his blade at me. I stumbled back against the wall and crashed painfully into a rack of weapons. Rolling aside, I yanked my stage sword awkwardly from its hanger and brought it to broad ward.

"Fool!" Nick swung at me again. I should have cried out for help, but I still feared that, if cornered by the company, Nick would reveal my connection with Falconer. Poor swordsman that I was, I would have to stop him myself.

I beat his blade aside and, from long habit, replied with a thrust. Nick warded it effortlessly, then aimed a swift cut at my head. Instead of warding it, I ducked and came up under his blade with my own. The blunted tip glanced off his ribs and knocked the play book from his grasp. With a growl of rage and pain, he set upon me in earnest, battering aside my defenses until he found a breach and delivered a quick, angry thrust. His point was not blunted, as mine was. It struck me just above the belt.

I staggered back, clutching the spot, staring in dismay at the blood welling from between my fingers and coursing down the front of my breeches. Nick was as stunned as I. His face went white, and he backed up a few steps, his eyes wide with surprise and alarm. In the next instant, he recovered enough to scoop up the play book and bolt from the room.

I collapsed on the lid of a trunk, gasping for breath but feeling no real pain yet, only a kind of numb panic flooding through my body. Footsteps pounded outside the room and Sander appeared in the doorway. "Holy Mother!" he breathed as he saw me slumped there, drenched in blood. "What happened?"

"Nick stuck me. 'A's getting away!"

"Let him." Sander crouched before me and tore open my doublet.

"But 'a's got the book!"

"Your life is more important—" Sander started to say. Then he halted, staring at my bloody belly.

"Is it that bad?" I asked. "Am I going to die?"

To my astonishment, he began to laugh. "You sot! He stuck your blood bag!"

"Me what?" And then it came to me. Nick's point had been stopped by the protective plate, and the only blood that had been spilled was that of an unfortunate sheep. Feeling sheepish myself, I struggled to my feet. "Come! We've got to catch Nick before 'a delivers that to Falconer!" I stumbled from the property room and ran headlong into Mr. Armin.

"Widge!" He stared at my gory costume. "What in heaven's name—?"

"It's naught," I interrupted. "Can you come wi' me, sir? Nick's stolen the book of *Hamlet*."

As I suspected, he was not the sort to waste time on words when action was wanted. "You're due on stage, Sander," he said, and we were out the door.

When we rounded the playhouse, I saw Nick, far ahead of us, heading for the river. So desperate was his flight that he had dropped his sword and not bothered to retrieve it. Mr. Armin paused long enough to snatch it up, thrust it in his belt, then set off again in pursuit.

I did my best to keep up, but I was hampered by the metal plate, which pinched my skin with every step. Mr. Armin glanced over at me. "Shouldn't you stay here? You're wounded."

I shook my head. "Sheep's blood," I said breathlessly, and he laughed in understanding.

By the time we reached the bank of the Thames, Nick had hired a wherryboat and was well out into the river. Mr. Armin sprang into a second boat, and swallowing my fear, I climbed in after him. "Catch that craft, and you'll have a shilling," Mr. Armin told the startled wherryman.

Had there been a choice, I'd have picked someone more muscular and less sickly-looking than the old sailor who propelled us into the current. When the play let out, the bank would be thick with boats, but at the moment, his was the only one.

To my surprise, our wiry wherryman, spurred on by the promise of more money, slowly closed the gap between Nick's boat and ours. When Nick turned and saw that we were gaining, he called something to his boatman and pointed. The boat abruptly changed course; instead of heading for the opposite bank, it swung downstream, in the direction of the bridge.

"A pest upon him!" Mr. Armin muttered. "He's going to shoot the bridge!"

"Oh, gis! 'A must ha' maggots in his brain!"

"Shall I go after?" our wherryman asked, not very eagerly.

"There's another shilling in it," Mr. Armin said.

I clutched frantically at my seat as the boat dipped and swayed. Then, catching the current, it surged downstream. Ahead, the river churned through the dozen stone arches of the bridge, as water in a smaller stream will boil between the fingers of one's hand, but with a volume and force a thousand times greater.

Nick's boatman steered toward one of the narrow archways. The boat was swept through like a leaf on a flood, bobbing wildly as the water beneath it struck the bridge supports and was flung away. One side of their boat banged and scraped sickeningly against the stone arches, but it emerged in one piece on the far side of the bridge.

" 'A made it!" I said, hardly knowing whether to be relieved or disappointed. In the next moment, I was neither; I was merely terrified, for our turn had come to shoot the bridge. Our boatman was either less skillful than Nick's, or less favored by the Fates. As the foaming mouth of the archway swallowed us, the stern of the boat swung sideways. Though the boatman thrust out his pole to try and keep us clear, we smashed against the stone support. The boat careened, and water poured over the gunwales, overturning it and spilling us into the rushing river.

The feeling of being flung into that whirling world of water is one I fervently hope never to experience again. Everything familiar and secure was snatched away and replaced by a single, suffocating element that robbed me of sight and hearing, of my very breath.

The seething water tossed me this way and that. I fought it madly, but it was as much use as fighting the wind. There was nothing to take hold of, nothing to kick out at. It took hold of me; it wrapped itself about me, dragging me deeper. When I gasped for air, it filled my lungs.

Curiously, even in my panic, a portion of my mind stood apart, observing my plight, as it had done during the performance at Whitehall. I'm going to die now, it said; how strange.

26

And then my flailing arms struck something solid. I had no idea what it was and cared less. My hands clutched it. Something grasped my chin and lifted it above the surface. I spewed out a pigginful of water and began to breathe again.

"Don't struggle, now," a voice said, sounding distant and muffled to my water-filled ears. "Try to relax." The voice was Mr. Armin's. "Kick your legs gently." I was accustomed to obeying his instructions, and I obeyed now. "Good, keep kicking that way."

There were more voices, then, and hands and boathooks snatched at our clothing and dragged us over the side of another wherryboat, which had apparently seen our plight and come to the rescue. When I had coughed up a portion of the river, I sat up and looked about. Mr. Armin sat next to me, breathing heavily, water streaming from his hair and clothing. In the bottom of the boat, our wherryman was stretched out, unmoving.

"Is 'a drownded?" I asked fearfully.

"No," said one of our rescuers. "More's the pity. It's swads like him give us rivermen a bad name."

"Well, he won't any longer," Mr. Armin said, "for his boat's gone to the bottom." He pulled his purse from inside his drenched doublet, took out two shillings, and pressed them into the unconscious man's hand. "As agreed," he said.

When our feet were on firm ground again on the north bank, we stood looking up and down, wondering what to do next. "Have you any notion of where Nick is likely to take the book?"

"I ken who 'a's taking it to, I just don't ken where."

Mr. Armin stared at me sternly. "I'll ask you to explain all this later. For now, I'll be content to get back the book. You think someone hired him to steal it?"

"Aye. A man named Falconer. The man you quarrelled wi' outside the Globe that day."

Mr. Armin nodded. "He's not a Londoner, is he?"

"Nay, sir. 'A hails from Leicester."

He frowned thoughtfully. "Leicester, is it? And you think he'll go there now?"

"Most like. 'A's not the sort to linger once 'a's got what 'a wants."

"He'll be leaving by way of Aldersgate, then. Perhaps we can head him off. Come." He shifted Nick's rapier, which he had somehow retained through our ducking in the river, and strode off. I had been in the process of unstrapping the protective plate. I yanked it off and hurried after.

Though I was free of that discomfort, I had a suit of clammy clothing to hinder me. In addition, I was close to exhaustion from my struggle with the river. Still, I trotted along in silence, not wishing to do or say anything irksome; my position was precarious enough already. "I'm sorry to be missing me part in the play," I said at length.

"They'll manage without you. This is more important."

"Does it matter so much an one company besides—besides yours puts on the play?" Besides *ours*, I was about to say, but I did not know whether or not they would still count me as part of the company after this.

"Of course it matters. It's wrong. No one has the right to the fruits of another's labor."

"Oh," I said. "I never thought of it that way."

"Besides, there are other concerns. Suppose this—What did you call him?"

"Falconer."

"Suppose this Falconer sells the play to a printer, who publishes it and has it registered. Then the Chamberlain's Men lose all legal right to perform it ourselves."

"Oh. I didn't ken."

"We generally delay publication as long as possible.

Some companies care little for registrations or rights, and to print the play is the same as saying 'Here it is, and welcome to it.' Yet if we *don't* publish it ourselves, someone will sell a pirated version. It's a tricky and an unfair business."

"Aye, I see that now." I felt more ashamed than ever of the part I'd played in the whole affair. I wanted to believe that we still might retrieve the play book, but knowing Falconer, I did not hold out much hope. Even if we did catch up with him, he was not likely to just apologize and hand it over.

By the time we reached St. Paul's and turned on to Aldersgate Street, I was sweating and trembling as if in the grip of the ague. But with the gate in sight, I managed to push myself yet a little farther. A ragged, legless beggar sat by the gate. Mr. Armin crouched and dropped a shilling into the man's filthy hat. "We want to know if you've seen a certain man pass by here. Describe him, Widge."

" 'A's tall and swarthy, wi' a black, unruly beard and a long scar on one cheek. 'A wears a dark cloak wi' the hood drawn up, and will have a brown horse, most like."

The beggar squinted thoughtfully, then shook his shaggy head. "Not as I recall, and I've a good eye and a good memory."

"We'll keep you company a bit, then," Mr. Armin said.

The beggar waved us away. "You'll have to sit somewheres else. No one gives aught to a beggar with well-dressed friends."

We sat on the far side of the gate, in the shade of an overhanging tree. I was grateful for the chance to rest at last, but I did not rest for long. Before five minutes went by, the beggar tossed a pebble at us to draw our attention and jerked his head down the street.

The beggar did indeed have a good eye. It was several moments before I saw the dark, cloaked figure leading a horse—the very figure I had been hoping, yet dreading, to see. I scrambled up, prepared to run. "It's him!"

Mr. Armin held out a hand to stay me. "Patience. Let's not frighten him off." He sat there, seemingly calm, until Falconer was nearly to the gate. Then he rose quickly to his feet and blocked Falconer's path.

Falconer did not appear in the least surprised or alarmed. "I thought we might meet again," he said, in that deep, rough voice.

"Really?" Mr. Armin replied. "I rather hoped we might not."

"Oh? I did not take you for a coward, sir."

"Nor am I, sir. It's not that I fear you, simply that I don't like you."

"You scarcely know me."

"That may or may not be. In any case, I have never liked thieves, and I suspect you are one."

Falconer dropped his horse's rein and pulled his cloak aside to reveal the hilt of his rapier. "No man calls me a thief—not more than once, at any rate."

"I did not say you were a thief. I said I suspected it. If I am wrong, I'll gladly tender an apology." He stepped casually to Falconer's horse and began to unlace the saddlebag.

Falconer drew his rapier. "Take your hands off that or I'll take them off for you—at the wrists."

Mr. Armin went on calmly unlacing the pouch. "I'll just have a look, and that will be that."

"Look well, then, for it will be the last thing you see in this world!" Falconer lifted his blade and brought it down, not upon Mr. Armin's head, as I feared, but upon the flank of the horse. The animal bolted. Just as suddenly, Mr. Armin's rapier left his side and came to low ward before him.

To my surprise, Falconer did not set upon him in the fierce and ruthless manner he had used to dispatch the band of outlaws. In truth, he seemed almost cautious. He tossed back the right edge of his cloak so it would not obstruct his sword arm, then grasped the other edge in his left hand and, with one deft movement, wrapped the hem of it twice around his forearm.

Mr. Armin seemed cautious, too, recalling no doubt their previous encounter, in which he had been so easily outdone. I know that I was recalling it. Though Mr. Armin was unquestionably an excellent fencing master, when it came to a duel fought in deadly earnest, I feared that he was no match for Falconer.

In such a situation, I had come to Julia's aid, and even Nick's, but this time there was nothing I could do, short of throwing myself upon Falconer's sword. Or was there?

What if I were to retrieve the play book? That was, after all, the reason behind the fight.

I dashed through the gate and looked about. Falconer's horse stood alongside the road a dozen yards off, grazing blithely, with no interest in his master's quarrels. But the moment I approached and reached for the saddlebag, he shied away, making me miss my footing and nearly fall on my face.

"Whist, now!" I called and moved in close again. Again he moved away. "The devil take you!" I muttered and approached once more. This time I got a firm purchase upon the saddle, and when the horse moved he pulled me with him.

He lashed at me irritably with his tail, then seeing he could not dislodge me, broke into a trot, dragging me along. Clutching the saddle frame with one hand, I plunged the other into the saddlebag, yanked out the play book, then dropped off onto the hard ground.

I limped hurriedly back to the gate, to find Mr. Armin and Falconer engaged in heated combat. "Stop!" I shouted above the clamor of blade upon blade. "Mr. Armin! I've got the book! Let's go!"

Mr. Armin stepped back and disengaged. "You go, Widge. I've unfinished business here."

"But there's no need for it now! I've got the book!"

Falconer pointed his sword at me. "Put it down, boy! I've enough of a score to settle with you as it is!"

"One score at a time," said Mr. Armin, and he closed in again.

"Stop!" I cried, more desperately. "Please! It's not worth it!" Neither man heeded me, if indeed they heard me above the din of their weapons.

I could not begin to describe their movements or strategies, so rapidly did they follow one upon the other. Their blades struck and warded and struck again with such speed that the eye could scarcely see them. Had it not been for their frantic clashing, I might have imagined they were not solid metal at all, but something thin and insubstantial, like the elder sticks we fought with as boys. If only it could have been so. If only they could have fought, as we did, until one adversary's weapon broke.

But this was a grown man's game, and the winner would not be the one whose weapon survived but the one who lived. And, I thought, clutching the play book to my chest, if that one proved to be Falconer, then what would become of me?

Mr. Armin had taught us in fencing class never to retreat from an opponent, for it is a defensive and not an offensive posture. He seemed to have forgotten his own advice. He was in almost constant retreat before Falconer's attack. I wanted to shout encouragement and instructions to him, as he had so often done to us. But even had my tight throat been able to form the words, I feared distracting him, so I watched in anxious silence.

Falconer grew more confident as the duel went on, pressing his advantage, driving Mr. Armin backward first one step, then another. Mr. Armin warded the blows easily enough but often failed to return them. Finally he found an opening and delivered an edge blow that would have sorely wounded Falconer except that he absorbed its force with the hem of his cloak.

In the same instant, Falconer stepped forward and thrust at Mr. Armin's unprotected chest. Mr. Armin spun aside, but not quickly enough. The point pierced his doublet and passed along his ribs, making him gasp in pain and stumble back. Falconer withdrew and thrust again, meaning to catch Mr. Armin unprepared.

But Mr. Armin was better prepared than he seemed. Instead of beating the blade aside, he performed a maneuver I had never before seen, and have not seen since. In truth, I thought it was a blunder. He fell forward, under Falconer's blade, and landed on his outstretched left hand, at the same time thrusting his sword before him, parallel to the ground. It took Falconer squarely in the belly and drove in halfway to the hilt.

Falconer gave a gasp of surprise and drew back. His hood fell away from his face, revealing his startled and scowling countenance. The skin of his face looked tight and twisted, as though something were pulling it askew.

He seized the blade of Mr. Armin's sword in his cloak-wrapped hand and, with a contemptuous gesture, jerked it free and flung it aside. For a moment, it seemed as though he had not been wounded at all. It was a trick, I thought, a collapsible sword. I half expected him to laugh and come at Mr. Armin again.

Then the blood began to well from the wound, spreading across his doublet, dyeing it red, and I realized with a shock that this was no illusion. This was not sheep's blood spurting from a bag, but his own life's blood draining away, and no amount of bandaging would staunch it.

Yet we had to try. Though Mr. Armin was bleeding himself from the gash under his arm, he stripped off his doublet and his linen shirt. We knelt next to Falconer, who had sunk onto the stones of the street, and tried to wrap the cloth about him.

He pushed it impatiently aside. "Let it be," he said in a voice so unlike his usual growl that I blinked in surprise. "It's no use."

Mr. Armin let the shirt drop and put an arm under Falconer's head as he sighed heavily and lay back. He seemed less like a man in pain than one who is simply unutterably weary. His face was weary, too. In full daylight, there was something curiously mask-like about his features.

He pressed a hand to his face, as though trying to hide it from our view, but his words said the opposite. "I suppose you have a right to see the true face of the man you've slain." As I watched in astonishment, he plucked at the dark skin of his cheek with his fingernails, and pulled away a great chunk of it. Where the repulsive scar had been there was now a smooth, pale patch of skin. Again his fingers dug at his face, and this time pulled away a portion of his hooked nose, leaving it straight and similarly pale-skinned. His eyes turned to me, and the look in them was almost amused. "You know me now?"

I swallowed hard. "Aye. Mr. Bass."

"And you?" he said to Mr. Armin. "But you knew before, did you not?"

"I suspected it."

"Still it was a good disguise, was it not? My masterpiece. Everyone's idea of what a Jew looks like, eh?"

"An excellent disguise," Mr. Armin said. "Such a talent should not be wasted."

"I agree. The very reason I left the Chamberlain's Men. There were too many fools in it to suit me."

"Better a company of fools than the company of thieves."

Mr. Bass coughed, and wiped the corner of his mouth. A bit of red smeared the back of his hand. "Perhaps so. But you must allow that I had the good taste to steal only from the best." Those were the last words he spoke, in this life at any rate.

Though death had taken my fellow orphans, and Dr. Bright's patients, I had never seen a man die at the hand of another, and had no notion of how I should react. I glanced at Mr. Armin, as if for a cue. He avoided my gaze and busied himself folding his doublet to prop up Mr. Bass's black-dyed head.

I had not shed tears in a long time, nor did I shed them now. All the same, I was overcome with a strange sadness, at odds with the relief I had expected to feel, now that the threat which had hung over me for so long was removed. The sensation was something like what I'd felt for Julia, when she had been forced to relinquish her position as a player. I could give no name to it, unless perhaps it was the word Julia had once tried to acquaint me with—compassion.

We sat with the dead man, ignoring the gawking crowd that had gathered, until a constable came and summoned a cart to bear the body away. The constable knew Mr. Armin, and when he was satisfied that the duel had arisen over stolen property, he let us go free.

We both had had our fill of the Thames, and so walked back to the Globe by way of the bridge. "How is it you kenned Mr. Bass?" I asked.

"I might ask the same of you. But I'd rather you told your story to the company as a whole, and let them judge you."

"Will they—will they turn me out, do you think?"

"I can't speak for them. As for how I knew Simon Bass—the truth is, I was with his company a short while before I came here. They were a sorry lot. Not only did they steal scripts, they often borrowed the name and reputation of some respectable company. They would give a single performance, then depart in the dead of night, often with the contents of the town's treasury. They seldom played the same town twice. There were scores of places where Bass dared not even go on legitimate business without disguising himself."

"But why bother to disguise himself from me?"

"I suppose he didn't want to risk your giving him away.

Or it may be he believed you'd follow orders better if they came from Falconer."

" 'A was right about that." I shook my head, still unable to quite understand. "But how could 'a bear to play a part for so long a time, and never reveal his true self?"

"Perhaps," Mr. Armin said, "it *was* his true self."

The Chamberlain's Men were more lenient than I expected or deserved. Both Mr. Pope and Mr. Armin argued on my behalf. Even Mr. Shakespeare, who had most cause to call for my dismissal, seemed inclined to forgive me. Only Jack spoke out against me, and not very vehemently.

So it was that I was permitted to stay on as a prentice with the company, and I was very grateful for it. I recognized now that I was being offered something more than just a career as a player, acting out a variety of roles. I was also being offered a chance at a real-life role, as a valued member of the Globe family.

My only cause for regret was that Julia had not been so fortunate as I. What had become of her no one seemed to know. Neither had we heard any news of Nick, but in his case no one cared much.

When several weeks went by with no word from Julia, Sander and I persuaded Mr. Armin to accompany us into the grimy depths of Alsatia, where we made a few inquiries. The man named Hugh recalled hearing that she was working as a serving maid for a household in Petty France, that colony of French émigrés just outside the walls of the city. Sander and I tried to track her down there, but neither of us knew enough French to make much headway.

All through the summer and into the fall, my schedule at the Globe remained hectic. In addition to all my new roles, I was given the task of copying out the individual sides from the book of each new play. Still I doubt that a day went by in which I did not think of Julia and wonder how she fared. I began to fear that she had joined her father at his unsavory trade and disappeared into the city's underworld, in which case we might despair of ever seeing her again.

Then, a week before Christmas, as we were preparing *Twelfth Night* for presentation at the court, Julia entered our lives again briefly, like the well-known Messenger I had so often played, who delivers his message and then departs.

Mr. Pope and Sander and I were on our way home after a trying performance, at which three so-called gentlemen took seats upon the very stage, thrust their feet in the players' paths, and distracted us with their "witty" comments. So busy were we venting our irritation that we scarcely noticed the serving maid who approached us until she spoke our names. "Widge? Sander?"

We halted and stared at her. "Julia?" I said.

She laughed at our looks of surprise. "Yes, it's me, disguised as a serving maid. Good day, Mr. Pope," she added, not very cordially.

Mr. Pope bowed slightly, as if to a lady—which, I had to

remind myself, Julia now was. "We've all been wondering what became of you."

"Nothing of any consequence, I'm afraid."

"That is unfortunate," Mr. Pope said, and I could tell that his words were sincere. "I truly wish that . . . that things could have worked out differently."

"So do I." Her tone was still far from friendly.

Mr. Pope cleared his throat uncomfortably. "Well. You'll want to talk with your friends, I expect. I'll bid you good morrow."

She made him a curtsy that was neither very graceful nor very gracious. When Mr. Pope was out of hearing, Sander said, "You might have been more kind. It wasn't his fault you had to go."

"I know that. It's no one's fault, really—or everyone's. It's just that I haven't quite gotten over it." She tossed her hair, which had grown long, and went on more cheerfully. "But I didn't come to open up old wounds. I came to tell you some good news, actually. It seems I may have the chance to be a player after all."

"Truly?" I said eagerly. "They've changed the rule?"

"No. No, I'm afraid not. But you see, Mr. Heminges once told me that in France women are permitted to act on the stage. So I've been working in the household of a French wine merchant, saving up my wages for passage money, and learning the language and—well, the long and short of it is, I sail for France in the morning."

"That's the good news?" I asked.

"Yes. Aren't you happy for me?"

"Oh. Aye. Of course."

"That's as happy as Widge gets, I think," Sander said, and shook his head. "Gog's bread, Julia, it's hard enough learning lines in English. How are you going to do it in French?"

She gave him an indignant look. "*Je parle français très bien, monsieur.*"

He laughed and held up his hands in surrender. "Very well, *mademoiselle*. If anyone can do it, it's you. Best of luck. I mean, *bonne chance.*"

"*Merci.*" She curtsied again, less awkwardly. "Widge? Aren't you going to wish me luck?"

"Aye," I said glumly. "Good luck."

She reached out and took my hand. "You needn't look so forlorn. Come, now, smile a little. For me?"

This business of friendship was a curious thing, I thought, almost as difficult to learn as the business of acting. Sometimes you were expected to tell the truth, to express your thoughts and your feelings, and then other times what was wanted was a lie, a bit of disguise. I was still but a prentice in the art, but slowly and painfully I was learning. Though in truth I felt more like crying, I put on the smile she asked for, or as near to it as I could come. "Up Yorkshire, we say 'Fair 'chieve you.' "

She squeezed my hand. "Fair 'chieve you, then." She backed away, as though compelled to leave, yet reluctant to let us from her sight. At last, she turned and hurried off in the direction of the Thames, which tomorrow would carry her to the sea.

As I watched her go, tears welled in my eyes, and for the first time since I was a child, I let them come. Now I understood why she had left us before without any farewell. Parting was not, as I had heard one of Mr. Shakespeare's characters say, a sweet sorrow. It was bitter as gall.

Behind us, Mr. Pope cleared his throat again. "She's a plucky girl."

Embarrassed, I wiped at my eyes. "She is that."

He put a hand on Sander's shoulder and mine. "We'd best be heading home now, boys. Goody Willingson has promised us toad-in-the-hole for tonight's repast."

"Toad-in-the-hole?" I said, laughing a little despite myself.

"Don't laugh," Sander said. "It's good. Almost as good as bubble and squeak."

"It certainly doesn't sound very good. But I can rely on your judgment, I suppose."

"You can that."

As the three of us—Mr. Pope and his boys—walked home, I reflected on these new terms and all the others I had learned—and unlearned—since my arrival here but a few months before. Though I hadn't quite learned a new language, as Julia was doing, I felt almost as though I had.

For every *ken* and *wis* and *aye* I had dropped from my vocabulary, I had picked up a dozen new and useful terms. Some were fencing terms, some were peculiar to London, some were the jargon of the players' trade. But the ones that had made the most difference to me were the words I had heard before and never fully understood their import—words such as honesty and trust, loyalty and friendship.

And family.

And home.